NISCENE'S CREED

NISCENE'S CREED

TIM GALLEN

This book is intended for MATURE audiences

To Nicole

First

"In the darkness, I bind my service. To Death, I pledge my fealty."

Though she heard other voices, Niscene E'terrall saw no one in the darkness. Not even the one who had brought them to this place.

"All I am and all I was is forfeit on the altar of Ash'a."

Suddenly, a bright flash of blue flame erupted in the front of the chamber. It nearly burned her eyes, but Niscene did not look away. She watched as the flame climbed higher, popping and hissing, until, as abruptly as it had burst to life, the blue flame died away, once again leaving the mysterious chamber cloaked in pure darkness. Niscene's life had been spent in darkness. Enough to incite fear in anyone. But she no longer feared it.

"From this day, the world will know not my face nor my name."

How he found her, she did not know. But he knew her face. He knew her name – and he knew every sordid detail of her wretched life. Every piece of pain and bit of betrayal. He knew it all, and she was afraid. When the shadowy figure approached Niscene in the dank, dark alley, her instincts told her to fight. But when she stared defiance into his eyes, fear seized her instantly, curling its fingers round her heart like a vice. Darkness no longer frightened Niscene E'terrall, but Ash'an Rah did.

Back in the chamber, Niscene glanced up from beneath her black hood. She scanned the front of the room where she knew he stood, shrouded in the inky darkness. Immediately, an unequivocal fear seized her. Her chest tightened and her mouth went dry. A violent shiver wracked her body. Finally, she averted her gaze and the fear ebbed.

"I shall leave no trace or memory of my presence in the world."

He knew of the Sense that sang to her on the margins of her mind, the mysterious melody that called to her from the penumbra of her consciousness. Such songs it sang. Songs of haunting and death, dark refrains of temptation and rage and chaos that played over and over in Niscene's mind. Songs that began as whispers in the dark when she was but a frightened little girl – and continued even after she first seized its power and made her tormentors burn.

"From the shadows shall I strike, and to the shadows shall I return."

He told her Ash'a, the Lady of Death, had heard her cries and sent him to offer salvation. He told Niscene the world owed her for what had happened. He said that he would help her. That Death Herself would help her. All Niscene had to do was pledge herself to the shadows. To disappear into the service of Death.

"From this day to my last I shall hold the world's fate in my hands."

She accepted his offer.

"I am a Bringer of Chaos."

A smile tugged at her red lips. Niscene's whole life had been full of chaos. Set upon her by her brother and his despicable friends. Chaos seemingly justified by the Maker or some other wretched god. But no more. With the power of the Sense and the promise of Ash'an Rah, Niscene E'terrall would repay the world for the torrent of pain and chaos in her life. Oh, yes.

"I am a Servant of the Lady of Death. I am Morad'ash."

For generations, the world has told stories to their children. Stories of hooded devils and shadowy figures who spread death and destruction throughout the land. Stories of the Morad'ash, who change the course of kingdoms with a word or blade or sorcery. Servants of Death Herself, who target kings and commoners alike. Children's stories. Told at festivals and during feast times. Intended to frighten. So children will behave. Children's stories. Nothing more.

As she spoke the final words, Niscene became very warm, as if kissed by a dragon. But then a shiver ran through her, chilling her to the bone. All the voices ceased. It was done.

"Morad'ash!" Like a volcano, Ash'an Rah's voice

erupted in Niscene's mind as if he inhabited it with her. Her mind began to burn and she could barely breathe. *"Your lives are forfeit to Ash'a. It is time to do Her bidding. Servants, rise."* Despite excruciating pain surging through her skull, Niscene mustered the strength to stand. As she did, she heard others climb to their feet, as well, though she saw no one – nothing but the inky darkness around her. *"It is time to serve our Mistress,"* Ash'an Rah's fiery voice hissed.

The fire in Niscene's mind died away, then, and small yellow flames winked to life on a thousand candles lining the chamber walls. A mixture of fear and exhilaration enveloped her. Fear of Ash'an Rah and the power he possessed. Exhilaration at the chaos she might bring. *I am a Bringer of Chaos.* The words of the Oath replayed in her mind. It was time to repay the world for all that had happened to her. To strike fear into the hearts of men. *I am Morad'ash.* The Sense hummed a haunting melody.

From under her black hood, Niscene noticed anonymous shadows file out of the chamber. How many there were, she could not tell. Only a few? Perhaps dozens? The hazy candlelight made it difficult to discern. Niscene looked at the front of the room. Ash'an Rah was gone.

Silently, she walked out of the chamber. Beyond, she shuffled along darkened corridors and hallways guided by only the flicker of small, tallow candles and their yellow flames that flickered from some unseen wind. The passageways she walked were dank and cool, but not bone-chilling; Niscene's nose wrinkled at some strange bitter scent she could not place. At the outskirts of her consciousness, the Sense called to her, as it always did.

She knew not how long she walked those corridors, but Niscene knew her quarters when she reached them. She entered, eager for – though uncertain of – what was next.

The room was simple and small, with a pallet and pillow for sleep, and a fireplace, which gave the room its only light. Someone had lit a fire, and the flames cracked and popped, and sparks jumped onto the hearth. Niscene gazed into the fire; her onyx eyes glistened as the flames danced before her, while shadows played games upon the walls like devils. A memory whispered to her from across time. In the fire she saw those who had wronged her. Their screams chorused in her ears, shouting for mercy, shouting for her to stop – promising, begging – up until the fire engulfed them. The Sense sang its terrible, beautiful song.

She reached out to seize it.

"Niscene E'terrall."

The voice of Ash'an Rah extinguished the memory and she retreated from the Sense. Her mind convulsed as if set ablaze, choking off all thought and breath. Unable to even gasp, Niscene slowly turned to face the hooded, shadowy, frightening figure who loomed over her.

"M-my lord," Niscene finally mustered through short, choppy breaths. She averted her gaze so as not to meet his eyes. Strangely, the Sense was silent, making her feel abandoned and alone. Afraid. Then, Niscene's head became warm, nearly feverish. She blinked and gasped at what she saw between open and shut. Amid the rising fever, she sensed a stirring, a summons. A command. *Look.* When she obeyed, two red dots peered at her from beneath the hood. The eyes of Ash'an Rah pulsed, turning an even deeper shade of red.

The flames of the fire flickered beside them, and out of the corner of her eye, Niscene glimpsed something atop the mantle. Without another thought, she reached up and snatched it from its perch. It was a rolled-up scroll of sandstone parchment. A black ribbon was tied around it.

Hesitant, Niscene glanced at Ash'an Rah, who stood, silent and ominous. He said nothing. No breath or word or syllable. She quickly looked away out of fear. Despite that fear and the fever pitch of her mind, Niscene's heart beat in anticipation. The only sound in the room was the occasional crack and pop of the fire.

Licking her lips, the newly minted Servant of Death held the scroll in her hand with an almost religious reverence. Fitting a finger underneath the black ribbon wrapped around it, she easily freed the slip of parchment. Unrolling it, Niscene held it close to the fire to read.

"She dies at the next full moon." His voice was like a thunderclap. *"Do what must be done."* His voice was fire and ice, thick with death and despair. *"Do not fail me. I will find you."*

The words pierced her heart like a cold knife, and she tensed, her shoulders tightening and her breath catching in her throat. Then, a thought came to her: *I will not fail.*

"I will not fail," Niscene said aloud, raising her head to look at her master. But she was alone.

The Sense called to her, then, its dark melody rising slowly from the edge of awareness. *I am a Bringer of Chaos.*

With one final glance at the slip of parchment in her hand, Niscene tossed it into the hungry fire.

SECOND

"WHAT IS YOUR business in the city?"

The guard asked the question without looking up at her. He sat behind a makeshift desk at the entrance to the capital city, Ramodin. In his hand, he held an ink-dipped pen, which hovered over a thick stack of parchment, which blew softly through the late afternoon breeze. The setting sun glinted off parts of his dinted armor. The guard's voice was a bored monotone, as if he had asked the same question a thousand times that day. Doubtless he had, considering the hours Niscene E'terrall had just spent queued behind any number of travelers, merchants, mummers, and caravans. And by the looks of the line that remained stretching down the great eastern highway – even as the sun had fallen to near halfway behind the great forest – he would ask a thousand times more.

Behind him, two mighty doors, fifty feet tall, marked the entry into the king's city. Immediately through them was a cobbled plaza, crowded with every manner of person. Farther on, the plaza became a street that led deeper into the capital. Niscene gazed longingly through the gates. *So close.* She had a rendezvous at sundown. It would not do to be late. The Sense sang to her one of its terrible melodies.

"The Midnight Court," she said, softly. She heard a few shallow gasps and under-the-breath comments from people behind her in line. The guard gave a start, fumbling the quill in his hand. A large dollop of ink flowered on the top piece of parchment and the pen fell to the dusty ground. Mechanically, the guard leaned down, with a grunt, to pick it up. As he set the pen on the table, he slowly raised his head to look at Niscene. He had beady little eyes above a nub of a nose on a ruddy, rotund face. What hair he had left was matted to the top of his head. His tiny dark eyes sized up the auburn-haired woman in front of him, as if evaluating a piece of meat at market. Niscene suddenly felt exposed, which she was in a way, considering her attire – a tight, reddish-brown bodice that emphasized her modest bosom, over which she wore a thin, brown shawl, as well as a free-flowing, extremely sheer skirt made for easy lifting, or ripping.

A rush of memories flooded her mind as the fat bastard ogled her. Memories of similar looks and gazes from similarly fat, sweaty men; men who saw and wanted only her body.

A lascivious grin spread across the guard's thick, dry lips. He urged her closer. Niscene did not move. Inside, the rage swelled, hastened by the chaotic chorus of the Sense. *Never again,* she reminded herself. Never again would she allow herself to be caught in such things. She imagined seizing the Sense and cutting off the man's cock and balls and feeding them to him while he bled out from between his legs on the dusty ground. What would it be like to hear him scream like a midnight banshee as she sliced through his flabby, soft skin with but a gesture? To watch him whimper and grimace in pain as she forced him to choke down shriveled and bloody bits of his own manhood?

Oh, yes, the temptation was sweet, but Niscene gritted her teeth and pushed back against it. She could not. She must enter the city. *I am Morad'ash.* Niscene crossed her arms over her chest, pulling her shawl tighter, and narrowed her onyx eyes.

"My shift ends at sundown," the guard said eagerly. He gestured toward the setting sun in the east, behind Niscene. "I could meet you at the Rusty Wagon Wheel just outside the Court." He licked his lips and a lustful hunger flashed in his round, little eyes. "Show you what a real man's got betwixt his legs." He chuckled as he jumped up from his seat. He grabbed at his crotch.

A handful of people queued behind Niscene grumbled and complained. One even yelled and cursed at the guard to just let her pass. But the corpulent fool ignored the grousing and muttering of the increasingly impatient crowd waiting their turn to enter the king's city. "What do you say?" he asked, a wide grin splitting his fat face.

Never in a thousand lifetimes, you pathetic creature, Niscene thought to herself as she regarded the man beneath the rapidly setting sun. She cocked her head in a manner she thought flirtatious, then forced her lips into a pout and sighed a disappointed sigh.

"Oh, Sir, how I am sorry; I've already an appointment for the evening," Niscene said. Doing her best to play the part, she slinked up next to the man, leaning in so her red lips nearly touched the man's cauliflower ear. "Perhaps another time," she whispered.

Without another word, she strode past the guard and made her way to the city gates. Straight ahead, she could see through them, into Ramodin; all the people and bustle, the massive palace looming over everything. Somewhere within lay her target. She only needed to continue walking a few more feet.

But suddenly the guard brought up a beefy hand to her chest and forced her back, away from the gate. "Where do you think you're going, *whore?*"

Niscene stiffened, and all at once she heard the memory of a hundred voices echo in her mind: *"You little whore, come here!" "You're nothing but a whore, you hear me?" "On your back, whore!" "The gods have forgotten you, whore!" "Where do you think you're going, whore?"*

"What did you call me?" she asked, when the flashbacks faded. She felt anger building inside of her. The

Sense sang one of its terribly haunting songs.

"You see, his majesty, King Paeter, don't care much for too many *whores* in his great city," the guard pontificated, ignoring her question. He then folded his bulky arms across his wide chest and stared at her with a sinister gleam in his beady, little eyes. He made a harsh, guttural sound then spat a large glob of greenish spit on the ground beside her. "Of course," he added, again grabbing himself between his legs. "Something could be arranged."

Niscene's eyes flicked from the man's face to between his legs and back. Her lips twisted into a devilish grin. "I suppose you're right," she said.

All at once, Niscene brought up her knee – connecting right between the man's legs. His face contorted into a pained grimace and he let out a howl of pain before collapsing to the ground and pulling himself into a ball, whimpering. Several women in line behind her hooted and hollered, while some men shouted insults and let out big belly laughs. Niscene glared down at the guard, writhing about, pitifully, in the dirt. She kneeled next to him. "If you call me whore again," she snarled, "I shall do far worse."

Still in pain, the guard managed to twist his head

round so he could stare daggers at Niscene. Through gritted teeth, he growled at her: "Fuck…you…*whore!*"

Now you've done it. Enraged, Niscene seized the Sense, its murderous melody piercing her ears. Its magik flooded every pore of her being, filling her with a pleasure unlike anything else in existence. With enhanced strength, she clutched the man's fat face in her hand. "You were warned," she hissed.

Letting go of the man's face, she got to her feet, then began walking into the city. Ahead of her lay the crowded plaza and busy streets of Ramodin. Behind her, Niscene heard the confused murmurs of those still queued at the gate, and the heavy, stunted breathing of the guard who dared call her a whore.

A moment later, she heard the screams, followed by cries for help and shouted prayers. She continued walking until the crowd just inside the gate swallowed her. Only then did she turn to take in the budding chaos at the gate. The fat guard had managed to lift himself to his knees, but blood spewed and spurted from his mouth. It cascaded down his formerly pristine, white armor and puddled on the dirt below. From somewhere, a trio of similarly garbed guards raced to their fellow. The strangeness of the scene seemed to rile up the line of pilgrims, merchants, and travelers waiting to enter the city.

In fact, for the moment, the gate to the city was unprotected. Niscene laughed as a group of blue-attired pilgrims seized upon the opportunity and rushed through it, into the capital, no doubt emboldened by the hours spent waiting queued to seek entrance. They sprinted past the small coterie of guards who circled their choking compatriot, shouting for them to halt. Soon enough, all who wished entrance to Ramodin began to converge on the city gates.

One of the guards shouted for everyone to stop but the crowd was too large and wild. While some of the guards tried to tend to their dying fellow, others got caught up in the impending riot and crushed underfoot by the stampede of people and carts and horses.

The scream of unsheathed steel pierced the air. Women wailed and fights broke out between everyone and the gate guards. A party of riders urged their horses onward, trampling over guards and other travelers alike. The screams echoed down the cobbled street.

Those already inside the gates turned to see what was the matter. People jostled Niscene as they ran by, but she minded not a bit, laughing at the entire scene. She had eyes only for the chaos at the gate, and the corpulent guard who spat up his final bits of blood. Street vendors and merchants ran indoors and other city dwellers tried to follow, hoping to get away from the growing riot. From further in the city, a unit of knights tried to make their way through the crowds toward the gate.

Still pulsing through her veins, the Sense sang its tumultuous melody as Niscene faded into the crowd, wading her way slowly further into Ramodin itself.

Eventually, the cacophony ebbed and the crowd thinned out. Soon enough she walked at a leisurely pace, the noise and maelstrom of the gate long behind her. Such action taken was risky, to be sure; the words of the Oath replayed in her mind like a chorus or creed. *But no one calls me a whore,* Niscene reminded herself. *Not anymore.* The Sense hummed its agreement.

THIRD

A FILTHY MESS, Ramodin.

Situated at the foot of the great Mountain at the End of the World, Ramodin, the capital of the Unified Kingdom, stretched like a yawning god along the base of the jagged, craggy peak, whose top was obscured by clouds and distance. Set into the mountain itself, the king's palace loomed, with its towers and spires stretching skyward, attempting in vain to match the mountain's summit. The palace, made of a smooth blue stone, shimmered in the disappearing sunlight.

Niscene maneuvered through the dense, sprawling

city, whose ancient, tortuous brick and cobbled streets twisted and turned, widened and narrowed. The ancient city's streets were dusty and dirty, filled with horse shit and crowded with people who smelled far worse: vagabonds, rapers, thieves and sellswords. Niscene scowled from under her shawl and wrinkled her nose at the disgusting concoction of scents and odors. Even the bloody nobility – those who traipsed about in fine silk clothes with their noses high in the air – stank in their way. Those of a higher station always did.

Though she had left behind the brutish guard at the city gate, Niscene still attracted unwanted attention as she maneuvered through the dense, sprawling capital. City Patrolmen, fingering weapons at their hips, skulked about, calling her far more wretched names than even the brute at the gate. Arrogant knights stared down at her from their slow-moving mounts as she walked by. Hungry gazes from other men, wearing rags and fine clothes alike, lingered as Niscene passed, while scandalized women shot disgusted looks in her direction. Even a blue-robed Philosopher frowned at her as she strode by on the flexuous brick and cobbled streets; his penetrating eyes judged her, righteously unaware of what she could do to him despite his piety.

The sweet chaos of the Sense whispered to her like a lover, calling to her over the din of the city at dusk.

They all knew where she was headed. The only place one attired such as she would be: the Midnight Court.

Found in the heart of the city, the Midnight Court catered to the realm's lords' and ladies' deepest, darkest fantasies and fetishes. The Midnight Court: where the rich and powerful came to forget their high-born station and allow their desires to overwhelm them. The thought of the place made Niscene want to retch.

As the light of day faded, Ramodin's streets alighted with the glow of street lamps, enchanted by some magik that triggered as the shadow of night came over them. Their light gave the streets a haunted air.

When the last patches of sunlight finally vanished in the eastern horizon, Niscene entered the Midnight Court. With night fully upon the city, the streets in the Midnight Court quickly took on a crimson haze. Overhead, the half moon glowed a ghostly white. The air grew dense with a sweet scent of roses and something Niscene could not place. *Filth*, she finally decided. She nearly gagged. The

Sense hummed its soothing melody.

As if by magik, the sidewalks and streets and buildings came alive with the sounds of decadence. Purveyors of fantasy and desire called from their doorsteps and street corners to the growing swarm of finely dressed people swelling in the streets. Their faces were obscured by leather masks of black or white.

With eager grins, those in masks approached those without. But quickly that eagerness turned to hesitancy as they awkwardly bent their bodies in bows and curtsies, kissing the offered hands of those whom they approached. Once so claimed, those without masks were led away by those wearing them, who casually slipped their hands into the others', whispering secrets and fantasies into their ears.

One group of large, white-masked men chased down a pair of black-masked women and took them right in the street, lifting high their skirts and ripping away their bodices. The women's cries for help soon melted into moans of ecstasy.

Niscene lingered a moment, disgust painted on her face, as she observed the scene. For the briefest of moments, she remembered a time she, too, had been taken by force. It was not that long ago, in truth. Her skin crawled as she recalled the feel of the calloused hands that held her down, and the terrible scent of fish on the man's breath. The triumphant gleam in his grey eyes when he had finished and thrown her to the ground to be discarded and forgotten.

Back in the Midnight Court, one of the masked men noticed Niscene and leered at her. There was a glint in his eyes. The Sense called to her then, its song terrible and sweet.

With a scowl, she strode by. The soft whimpering moans of the women fading away behind her.

As she stepped deeper into the Midnight Court, past ever-more iniquitous scenes, hands stretched out from the crimson shadows, groping and caressing. Sweet, soft voices called to her, asking to play and tease and more.

"Away with you!" she hissed, shrugging away from the disembodied limbs that reached for her.

When one hand nearly slipped between her legs, Niscene's fraying patience finally severed. The Sense howled with delight as she seized it and slit the fingers that violated her. Blood splattered in all directions and a pained shriek filled the air. Niscene did not stop. A smile tugged at her lips as the sweetness of the Sense pulsed through her body.

Turning at the next corner, she came to a building whose front was made entirely of glass. A small crowd of people huddled in front of the building, watching dozens of naked men and women on their hands and knees. They wore black masks, beady eyes gazing out through tiny slits; red welts and strips of blood marked their otherwise flabby, pale skin. Standing over them, leather-clad, tattooed women and men brandished whips and sharper things yelling and belittling the submissive nobles between blows. The blood-curdling screams that emanated from the transparent establishment shook the glass and tickled Niscene's skin.

She watched a while, strangely curious as to why some high-born noble – or anyone – desired such humiliation.

She soon saw two girls – barely flowered by the look of them – impossibly thin, naked, and kissing in the street. Their hands caressed each other up and down, moaning and whimpering softly. With haunted eyes, they looked up at two men in fine red and blue coats standing nearby. The men wore black masks and watched the young girls with hungry smiles. They tossed coins at them, and laughed as the tiny things scrambled after the gold and silver that clinked along the cobbles.

In that moment, the pain Niscene knew all too well returned. A burning sensation erupted between her legs before anger stuffed it out. *Dirty, rotten, bloody monsters!* Niscene clenched her hands into fists. The Sense hummed its sweet song as it flowed through her. Oh, how she wished she could stab them in their eyes. *That would wipe the despicable grins from their faces.* The thought brought a smile to her lips. But she had tarried long enough. She had an appointment to keep, after all.

With much difficulty, she let go of the Sense, clenching her teeth at the sudden loss. She took a deep breath and continued along the cobblestones; the two men's laughter echoed behind her as another handful of coins tinkled along the street.

Though much of the debauchery was flaunted, the Midnight Court was known for extreme discretion and secrecy. Lords and ladies wore masks of white and black to hide themselves in plain sight. Despite this, Niscene knew her appointment on sight.

Of average height, she stood alone on a street corner, black leather mask concealing her face. Casually, she held her hands clasped in front her, perhaps waiting for a carriage or a servant rather than a pleasure mistress. Long locks of strawberry blonde hair fell across her shoulders in waves. She wore a beautiful purple gown that looked dark blue in the crimson night. It was a dress better suited for a palace ball than the scantily clad alleys and back rooms of the Midnight Court. As Niscene approached, a duo of passing men attempted to draw her attention with words both sweet and sour.

"Oh, pretty lady, we shall show you pleasures unlike any you have known," teased one while the other performed an obscene gesture on the sidewalk, a wide, oily smile on his face. "Come, come, come with us, lovely, lovely lady."

They danced around her for a bit, gyrating and thrusting their hips and other bits at her. Then each man extended a hand, palm down, toward the woman. She made no motion to examine them. She gave a sharp shake of her head. The men made a few more obscene gestures and expressed their displeasure before skulking away down the street.

As the paramours stalked away, Niscene approached, drawing the blonde woman's attention. She stared at her with a haughty detachment, but said nothing. A pair of sharp, blue eyes watched as Niscene stopped beside her. Silent, without acknowledgment, the woman stared – confident, calculating, covert. Her eyes were unused to being met. But Niscene E'terrall had looked into the darkness that was the face of Ash'an Rah. She had peered into the black void from which no light escaped. She met the woman's gaze.

And waited.

Custom of the Midnight Court dictated that the patron publicly acknowledge and accept a purveyor for the evening. Yet, the blonde, masked woman stood stock still, sharp eyes regarding Niscene with slight annoyance. The wantonness of the Midnight Court ebbed and flowed, thrumming like the beat of a drum around them, but still both women simply stared at each other.

Niscene grew impatient. *Well, woman? What are you waiting for?*

Finally, the masked woman let out an exaggerated sigh. Then she dropped a perfunctory curtsy to Niscene, who was taken aback by such an action. With back still bent, the woman grabbed for Niscene's hand, handling it with a firm, yet gentle, grace. She kissed it. The Sense hissed, as though scandalized. Niscene herself nearly flinched. The brief kiss was wet and soft, unlike most kisses she had known. Still, she wanted nothing more than to pull her hand away. Her skin crawled and she stymied a shiver and scowl. Niscene despised physical touch. Yet she forced herself to accept the gesture. After all, it was what she wanted, what she needed to happen.

When the woman pulled away her lips, she stood up straight. Her lips curled into a thin smile, though her blue eyes were unreadable. Still holding Niscene's hand, she gave a soft squeeze and then led her down the street, further into the Midnight Court. They fell into a leisurely pace, as if they were two old friends out for an evening stroll. Niscene's hand twitched and she bit her tongue, fighting every urge to pull her hand away.

The sounds of debauchery emanated from the Court's red shadows but Niscene was fixated on the woman beside her. *It truly is she,* Niscene thought, her heartbeat quickening its already rapid pace. *And I am to kill her.* A grin tugged at her lips. She glanced upward at the half moon in the sky. The fiery command from Ash'an Rah echoed through her: *"She dies at the next full moon."* Despite the still air, Niscene shivered.

Soon, the masked woman stopped in front of a nondescript stone building.

When they entered, hushed voices quieted. Three people, an unmasked man with long, greasy hair and two white-masked women, stood inside the door. Two lanterns hung on either side of the wall, giving off a dull light. Niscene's nostrils twitched at the familiar scent of smoke and sweat and sex. The women briefly glanced each new arrival up and down before turning away and falling into indiscernible whispers. With a questioning look, the greasy-haired man raised five fingers and Niscene's black-masked companion nodded. In the lantern light, greed flashed in the man's eyes. His lips curled into an oily grin. He extended an open palm.

Without hesitation, the blonde woman pulled a small purse from between her bosom and set it in the man's hand. He hefted it, then nodded. Turning around, he reached into a dusty, broken cupboard that hung on the wall and pulled out something that glinted when the dim lantern light caught it. He handed it to the masked woman, who grabbed it and placed it down her dress.

Without a word, she squeezed Niscene's hand and took her down the hall toward a set of stairs, barely visible from the dull light at the front of the hall. The woman began ascending the steps, still holding Niscene's hand. The wooden stairs groaned beneath their soft footfalls.

When they reached the top, the woman led Niscene down a hallway as dimly lit as the foyer downstairs. They passed doors, behind which could be heard muffled moans and other sounds of iniquity. The only light came from a few lanterns strewn along the walls. Even inside, the ubiquitous red haze of the Midnight Court persisted.

The women stopped at the door at the end of the hall. From down her dress, the blonde woman drew what the man downstairs had handed her: a small iron key. She inserted it in the lock and turned it. The lock clicked and she pushed open the door, which creaked softly.

She ushered Niscene inside and shut it behind them.

Pale moonlight shone through a thinly curtained window at the back of the small room.

The blonde woman moved with familiarity. As her eyes adjusted, Niscene saw her stop in front of a small vanity in the corner. A second later, a small flame burst to life and she lit a tallow candle. Picking it up, she turned to face Niscene; the woman's face glowed in the soft light.

"I have paid for the week," she said.

"Of course," Niscene answered.

"I hope to take full advantage of it," the other woman continued. She arched an eyebrow. "If you're as good as your reputation suggests."

Niscene stiffened, but said nothing. She knew not what to say. The pleasure mistress whose throat she slit a day earlier took most of her secrets with her, including her newest client's fetishes and fancies. Clearly, Niscene's target enjoyed the company of women. But in what fashion? Her stomach twisted in knots at the thought of what she might have to do.

"Undress me," the woman commanded. Not waiting for acknowledgment or response, she set down the candle and approached Niscene. Turning her back, she pulled her strawberry blonde hair over her shoulder.

"Yes," Niscene said. "Of course." Licking her lips, she stared at the nape of the woman's neck. She hesitated.

"I asked if you would undress me," the woman said, her voice thick with annoyance. Niscene bristled at the outburst and the Sense howled on the fringes of her mind. Through clenched teeth, Niscene slowly lifted her hands. To calm herself, she imagined that, instead of undoing the buttons on her dress, she wrapped her hands around the woman's dainty, pale neck, slowly tightening, cutting off her air, wringing the life from her, applying her full strength when the woman began to thrash about – watching with maniacal glee as the light faded from her blue eyes.

From the edge of consciousness, the Sense sang its terrible song and Niscene's lips twitched. Eyes widening in the darkness, she mouthed the words of the Oath: *From the shadows shall I strike.*

And why not? What was stopping her? After weeks of travel across the realm, after hatching the perfect plot, after taking the place of the true pleasure mistress, dressing in her scandalous attire, and entering the city: here she stood – inches from the woman she was sent to kill. Why bother with the charade? Why not kill the woman now, strangle the life from her, and be done with it? Why wait for the full moon at all? *I am a Servant of the Lady of Death.*

"I often enjoy such preludes," said the woman with a sigh. The annoyance raised Niscene's ire to near boiling. *Oh, I will so enjoy killing* you. With a scowl, she finally touched the woman's neck. At her touch, the woman seemed to tremble as if in anticipation. She sucked in a short gasp of air. It was difficult for Niscene to see the woman's dress. But after fumbling her hands about a bit, she soon found the mix of buttons and knots. With perfunctory action, she began undoing them.

"Rather hasty, aren't you?" the other woman said, annoyance still thick on her words as she shrugged off her gown. It fell to the floor in a heap. "But, very well." Slowly, she stepped out of the pile at her feet and turned toward Niscene. In spite of herself, Niscene lowered her eyes to gaze at the other woman's naked body. It was unlike some of the others she saw earlier on her stroll through the Midnight Court. Shapely, trim, and firm; no question the woman qualified as beautiful.

"Don't be shy," the woman said, stepping closer.

What annoyance there had been, heavy in her mouth, melted away, replaced by a honey-like sweetness. "Do you like what you see? Most do." Wearing nothing but the leather mask on her face, the woman's lips twisted into a thin smile.

"Touch me," she cooed. Niscene gave a start. She had not expected such a command – request? She swallowed and stood staring, frozen in place. With a light laugh, the woman reached for Niscene's hands. She lifted them and pressed them firmly to her breasts. "I do not mind."

Despite herself, Niscene licked her lips and began to hesitantly move her hands across the woman's chest and down her midsection.

"Shall we take this to the bed?" the woman asked. "Perhaps you will shed your tentativeness there."

Clutching Niscene's hand, she led her to the bed that sat in the middle of the room. When they stood next to it, a sliver of something caught Niscene's eye. Above the bed something swayed gently; she heard the faint creak of disused metal. Her onyx eyes found the outline of whatever hung above the bed. Chains? Yes, and more. Niscene's eyes widened. The Sense hummed as it, too, understood. With a sidelong glance, Niscene looked at the other woman.

"Fasten my hands?" she asked. The words sounded awkwardly submissive, as if the woman were not used to speaking in such a manner. Without waiting for a response, she stepped up onto the bed, then held out her hands.

Recalling what she had seen earlier, Niscene felt her lips twist into a diabolical grin. Scenes of naked masked men and women, beaten and bloody, replayed in her mind. The screams, the howls; the pleasure that was pain. As always, the Sense sang its haunting melody.

"It would be my pleasure," she said.

Cold, heavy, and rusted, the fetters whined softly when Niscene clasped them around the woman's wrists. She let out a soft gasp when they clicked in place.

"Are you going to hoist me?" the woman asked. "The lever is over there, by the window." She tilted her head toward the back corner of the room. Hidden in shadow, Niscene saw a metal lever and mechanism. Like the manacles themselves, It was cold and rusty, but worked well enough after she loosened it. Chains rattled and the gears groaned a portentous sound as Niscene turned the lever.

With each turning, the trammels tightened, eventually

becoming taut enough to pull the woman's arms above her head until she hung mere inches over the bed, her toes barely brushing the sheets.

Niscene wore a dark smile as she strode to the bed, gazing up at the very vulnerable, very naked woman hanging above it. *I could kill you now,* she whispered in her mind. The Sense purred at the thought. *Yes,* she continued, nearly seizing the Sense. She reached out, placing a solitary finger at the inside of the woman's left knee, then dragged it upward like a knife across the thigh. The leg muscle twitched and she moaned. "Please," she begged. "The whip."

Whip? Niscene had not seen a whip. "On the back wall," her target whimpered, almost pleading. Finding it and retrieving it, she resumed her teasing. Unrolling it, she took one end in each hand and wrapped it around the woman's waist, sliding the leather whip up under her breasts then down to her feet. The woman moaned softly. Niscene wanted to retch.

"Be gentle at first," the woman said when Niscene ceased the foreplay and positioned herself, whip at the ready. "It has been a while since I've had the pleasure."

"Of course," Niscene said. "Your majesty."

FOURTH

"None of that," said the queen of the realm. "With this mask on, I could be anyone."

Niscene nearly laughed. *Of course you could. But you're not.* Despite the black mask that obscured her face, it was clear as a summer day the naked, vulnerable woman, whose hands were fettered in chains, was E'lisea, queen of the realm, mother to the royal children, and faithful wife to King Paeter.

Although, perhaps not so faithful.

"My *d'ongrata* is Paeter," the queen whispered.

So sweet, thought Niscene as she flicked the whip

against the wooden floorboards. The action drew a soft moan from the queen, followed by a shiver that jostled her chains. A smile tugged at Niscene's lips, and her timidity began to fade. When she again cracked the whip upon the floor, the queen's body tensed and her breathing quickened. "Oh!" she gasped. Niscene's eyes regarded the helpless, naked woman hanging overhead. She began to circle the round bed, teasing the queen, running the cool leather of the whip along her skin, occasionally snapping it against the wooden floorboards. Each loud *crack* elicited another shudder of anticipation.

Embracing her part in this play, Niscene awkwardly jumped up on the bed. With her free hand she grabbed the queen's face. The woman's blue eyes flashed with terrible excitement and anticipation. Then, Niscene squeezed. For her part, the woman's breathing quickened, but she made not a sound. With a wicked smile, Niscene dug her nails into the queen's cheeks. Blood trickled out and down her fingers.

"You will know pain," said Niscene, her voice low and menacing. Somewhere on the fringes of her mind, the Sense stirred, and she squeezed more until the queen finally gurgled in pain. Niscene let go, then whispered, "Like none you have ever known."

"P-please," the queen begged, all her earlier arrogance vanished. "Gods, please."

The Sense stirred once more. At first, its melody was soft and low, a faint murmur in the darkness. How quickly its music rose, calling out with its promise of pain and chaos. Niscene licked her red lips. *I am a Bringer of Chaos.* If the woman wanted pain, thought Niscene, she would deliver it.

In the hazy light of the room, the whip cracked like lightning bolts across the queen's body. Her screams and cries, a mix of pleasure and pain, shook the room like thunder in the night.

"Oh, sweet gods!" cried Queen E'lisea. "Please! Do not stop! Oh!" In response, Niscene cracked the whip afresh against the woman's soft, nude body. The Sense sang louder with each blow, nearly begging Niscene to seize it.

Niscene again cracked the whip, and its leather fingers welted the queen's flawless back. Soon, E'lisea's beautiful body became red and raw. Her strawberry hair was thick with grime, and greased with her own blood.

Still, she cried for more.

At the edge of her own consciousness, Niscene reached toward the Sense, still calling out to her. The closer she came, the more intense its call. With each crack of the whip and piercing scream of pleasurable pain from the queen, the more Niscene wanted to lose herself in the sweetness of the Sense.

Niscene heard the Sense crescendo with each of the queen's cries. A buzz began to hum in her own loins. Such a sensation summoned memories of her brother and his lecherous friends and the life she used to know. The Sense's song turned to screams. Niscene blinked and the queen became her brother, frightened and bloody. With each blow, he cried out. *"I'm sorry, sister! So, so sorry!"* Fierce anger took over, and Niscene's strikes became more violent.

Three hard blows drew out the strangest scream yet. The howl of pain and pleasure brought Niscene from her fantasy. Back to reality, she struck the queen. One of the whip's cords wrapped around E'lisea's back, making contact with her breast, causing her to lurch about like a hooked fish.

Still, she begged for more.

"Please!" the queen screamed. "More! Oh, *gods*!"

Like drink or drug, the woman's screams and moans intoxicated Niscene; a warm sensation ran up and down her body. The Sense buzzed and hummed and rattled her very being. *Yes*, thought Niscene. *Oh, yes.* Enough preamble. No more delay. It was time. The call of the magik mixed with the queen's piercing screams became too much. The sweet and haunting melody of the Sense became deafening. Reaching out, Niscene seized the Sense, its sweet magik and power seeping into her. *I am a Bringer of Chaos.*

Niscene exploded with magik and chaos; her senses sharpened, amplified by the torrent of power. She heard the rapid beating of the queen's heart, every ebb of her heavy, labored breaths. She smelled the familiar, pungent scent of sweat and blood that hung in the air, overwhelming the dead staleness of the room. In the hazy, vermilion darkness, her vision was clear and focused, revealing the innumerable bloody stripes and blemishes along the queen's body, shimmering like red rivulets down her back.

Through the swarm of power that filled her, Niscene heard, sharp and clear, the queen's voice, raw and astonished: "The Sense? You—you hear the Sense?"

The woman's words were like ice, instantly smothering the inferno inside Niscene. She shuddered softly as the intoxicating sweetness of the magik winked out. Her eyes widened in shock then her shoulders slumped. She shuddered at the sudden, jarring emptiness inside her. She even let out a soft whimper. The whip slipped from her hand, landing with a loud thud on the cold, wooden floorboards. Shaken and weak, Niscene, too, collapsed to the floor – the world again dull and listless.

Above her, the queen let out short, shallow breaths. She sucked in air like a woman close to death. Her shackles whispered softly as she swayed. "Why…" the queen wheezed, her voice raspy and lethargic. "Why not tell me?"

Because it is how I will kill you, thought Niscene, still reeling from the abrupt loss of the Sense. *On the full moon. I am Morad'ash.* She groaned as she pressed her eyes shut. On the fringes of her mind, she heard the Sense, singing as it always did. To seize it was like attempting to tame a thunderstorm. To lose her hold of it so suddenly left her dizzy and disheveled, a pathetic, helpless babe whimpering on the floor. Niscene clenched her jaw, then shook her head, attempting to clear it.

"I, too, hear the Sense," said the queen.

Niscene froze. "What did you say?" she asked, lifting her head to stare at the queen. E'lisea was bloody and beaten. The woman hung there, sweaty and slick, perhaps even near death. And yet? Niscene's onyx eyes narrowed to slits as she gazed up at the queen, looking deeper than her battered body.

How had she missed it?

"Yes," Niscene whispered, though more to herself. "There. I see it now." And she did. That familiar faint pulse that surrounded others capable of such clairaudience was clear. How *had* she missed it? Then the queen said the last thing she expected: "Would you...*use* the Sense?" Her tone was hopeful, almost pleading. "Instead of the whip?"

Niscene nuzzled a slippered toe against the whip at her feet, where it lay when she dropped it moments earlier. A smile tugged at her full red lips. The Sense's wicked song became louder in her ears.

She seized it.

The queen screamed.

FIFTH

NISCENE WAS UNSURE which she enjoyed more: the sweetness of the Sense coursing through her veins, or the viciousness with which she whipped the queen – who begged for more.

With each measured blow, her majesty's screams pierced the air, nearly shaking the pleasure house's very foundation. With each crack of air against her body, the bed over which the queen hung turned a deeper shade of red.

Niscene still could not believe she failed to see the other woman's propensity for magik. *And yet she insists I make her scream like some pathetic whelp.* She struck the queen's bottom, a blow that also caught her between the legs. E'lisea's head snapped back as though wrenched by an unseen hand; her breath caught in her throat before she coughed out something more than just blood.

"P-Paeter!" she cried. "Paeter!"

So lost in her duty as pleasure mistress, it took Niscene a moment to comprehend. The *d'ongrata*. Through gritted teeth, she ceased the beating. Like a whirlwind, the Sense flowed through her, its magik and power and chaos swirling. She ran a hand across her brow, brushing away specks of blood and sweat. If not for the Sense, she would have fallen to the floor, exhausted.

Above her, the queen wheezed. "P-please," E'lisea begged, coughing up fresh blood. "Ch...ch...chains..." she panted before her head went limp and rolled to the side. Without a word, Niscene waved a hand and the queen's shackles clicked open. Like a house of cards, the woman collapsed upon the bed beneath her, into a pool of her own blood. She sucked in small, raspy breaths, attempting to lift herself. But she could not.

Still clutching the Sense, Niscene stood beside the bed, passively observing the woman she had come to kill cling to life. *"She dies on the next full moon."* The words of Ash'an Rah rose up in her mind – as did his promise if Niscene failed: *"I will find you."*

All of a sudden, the queen let out a long, thin gasp while her body shuddered as if Ash'a herself gripped her heart. A breath later, her majesty fell silent.

Time passed and the silence stretched on, engulfing the room. Still, E'lisea did not move.

Beside the bed, Niscene's eyes widened and her body convulsed in terror. Had she truly done it? Had she killed the queen too soon? The crumpled body was still in the darkness, unmoving and lifeless. Dead. Niscene ran to the window. Outside, the red haze of the Midnight Court had thickened into a heavy, dense fog. Through it she could just make out the dull, soft light of the moon – only days away from full – and knew she had failed.

Stumbling backward from the window, fear gripped her. Niscene lost her hold on the Sense and the emptiness overwhelmed her.

She had failed – but could she flee? She shot a quick glance from the queen's body to the locked door. Dawn still was far off. The queen would not be discovered for hours yet. If she left now, could she not make it to the forests north of the city? By nightfall, would she not be at the cliffs of World's End, with its howling winds and foamy waves crashing below? Surely, he would not follow her beyond the sea?

Suddenly, the room seemed to grow both warmer and colder at the same time, and darker; a wave of dread rose up to swallow her. Paralyzed by fear, Niscene held her breath. A soft something – a breath or wind? – pricked the back of her neck. She shivered.

Again the words of Ash'an Rah whispered to her: *"Do not fail me!"*

"No!" she cried out, arms flailing at the unknown specter behind her. But there was nothing.

Then, out of the darkness, there came a soft, raspy breath followed by the long drawing in of air to lungs, like the first breath of life.

On the bed, slowly, the queen moved; she tried to lift her head and shoulders but they fell back to the pool of blood in which the rest of her lay. Niscene rushed to the queen, relief flooding into her. *Gods be good! She's alive.*

Still, Niscene was unsure of what to do. E'lisea's

breaths were shallow and thin. She said nothing and moved little. Hesitantly, Niscene touched the queen's bloody shoulder, but she retracted from the gesture. "N...no..." the woman wheezed. The queen's body then began to glow. All around her a faint, blue-green light pulsed to life then instantly died away. Niscene watched, silent but awed, as the queen seized the Sense. In such a state, her body beaten and bloody, and very nearly dead, the woman ought not be able to muster the strength to hold onto the tempest that was the Sense – seizing it was like trying to tame a dragon. Yet, she did; and Niscene stared in amazement as E'lisea wielded and worked the magiks deftly, conjuring and working them all about her own body.

The magik washed over the queen, closing up her wounds, knitting her skin back together like a goodwife sewing a rag doll for her daughter. Like a balm, the magik renewed her, returned her to life. A notion suddenly struck Niscene. This queen was no mere haughty high-born nor milquetoast ma'am.

"Mmm...Maker's mercy," E'lisea sighed, sitting up on the bed. The floorboards creaked softly as she stood and stretched. In the dim candlelight, Niscene saw the contours of the woman's lean, naked body. Where moments before it had been bloody and bruised and beaten, now there was not a mark. Save for residual smears and streaks of dried blood, the woman's body was pristine. Perfect. Beautiful.

With one final stretch, the queen let out a noise like a cat's meow. "Oh, *gods!*" she exclaimed, dropping her arms to her side. With a contented sigh, she turned her eyes on Niscene.

"Your abilities are extraordinary," said the queen, admiring Niscene as one did a lover. "I've never known the pleasure of pain from magik before." She tossed back her head and moaned. "Gods, had I known you heard the Sense, I likely would have paid old Fabyle thrice what I did!"

With a light laugh, the queen slinked by Niscene, intentionally thrusting her hips into her as she passed. Niscene, who stood flummoxed, mouth slightly agape, recoiled at the gesture, eliciting a harder laugh from E'lisea.

"You are an odd one, mistress," said the queen, striding across the room. She stopped in front of a metal wash basin that sat in the corner. "Of course, if every night with you is like tonight, I'll gladly tolerate any quirk you may have."

E'lisea submerged her hands into the tub in front of her, then paused and glanced over her shoulder. "You may watch," she said. "I do not mind."

Still standing beside the bed, Niscene said nothing. She stepped toward the woman, then stopped awkwardly and tilted her head, confused. While she splashed water on herself, the queen regarded Niscene, her blue eyes gazing out from behind her black leather mask, bold and deep, even in the room's dull candlelight.

"I had my doubts at first," said E'lisea. "But your reputation is well warranted." Her thin lips twitched upward into a knowing smile.

Niscene frowned. How odd, this queen. Only moments removed from nearly dying in a pool of her own blood and now she simpered as if they were pillow friends exchanging secrets. More playful, more coy, more flirtatious. Niscene shook her head at the absurdity of it all.

And yet, strangely, her onyx eyes remained curiously fixed on E'lisea, watching her methodically clean herself, washing away the dried blood and sweat, performing the last act of restoring her body to its original, unblemished condition.

She next lowered her blonde curls into the water basin and slowly brought them out. Water droplets trickled back into the tub as she twisted and squeezed the strands like a towel. Even in the low light, the queen's hair shimmered when wet, catching some of the pale, rufescent moonlight peeking through the window behind her. Again, Niscene's eyes traced the shape and form of E'lisea's naked body.

The Sense called to her, singing its melody – but Niscene ignored it, strangely intrigued by the queen's bathing ritual and other things.

"Do you like what you see?" asked E'lisea.

Suddenly flummoxed, Niscene gave a start. "What?" she asked, lifting a hand to her cheek to hide the rising crimson. A spark of annoyed anger flashed inside of her.

"It is all right, mistress," said the queen, stepping out from behind the wash basin. She tilted her head, regarding Niscene with her bold blue eyes. "Our contract needn't be all pain and chains." E'lisea took a step, then another, until she stood inches from Niscene, whose heart felt as if it would burst right through her chest. Her breath caught in her throat and her nostrils filled with the sweetest scent. "If that is what you desire," whispered E'lisea. "All you must do –" their lips now nearly touched – "is ask."

Time seemed to slow down, but Niscene said nothing. Paralyzed with uncertainty, she could only stare into the queen's eyes. So blue, they were like deep oceans gazing out from behind the leather mask. Somewhere in the distance she heard the Sense calling to her in its beautiful and chaotic song. But she ignored it.

Then, time resumed its natural pace and the queen's eyes blinked. She stepped away, leaving Niscene stunned and feeling suddenly alone.

The queen strode over to the pile on the floor that was her gown. Kneeling down, she pulled up her dress in silence, throwing a coquettish glance at Niscene over her shoulder. "Will you help me dress, mistress?" she asked, gesturing to the mess of buttons and hooks that ran along the sides of her back.

"Yes, of course, your majesty," Niscene said, stepping up behind the queen. Again, she noticed the woman's sweet scent. It smelled of honeysuckle in early spring. Niscene wished she could inhale it forever.

The queen clucked her tongue and scoffed, playfully. "None of that, mistress," she said, her smile betraying the chastisement. "I am just some woman paying for the pleasure."

Are you? Niscene wondered as she buttoned and hooked the queen's gown. *And yet, you have been marked for death by Death Herself.* Niscene's mind swirled and swam with questions and speculations.

When she finished with the queen's gown, Niscene let her hands fall to her sides and stepped back. E'lisea smoothed out her skirt then turned to regard Niscene. "You are a strange one, mistress," she said. "Quiet and tentative, at times." She crossed her arms beneath her breasts and tilted her head. "Yet, you hear the Sense and wield it masterfully in the painful pleasures." The queen took a deep breath and wrapped her arms tight around herself, closing her eyes. Then she let out a shiver. When she opened her eyes she smiled a hungry smile. "I wonder: Will a week be long enough with you?"

Stepping out into the crimson night, Niscene shivered. The red haze that permeated the Midnight Court hung low and thick, chilling the early spring air. The fog was so heavy that the women were forced to step cautiously as they ambled along the cobblestone streets, with their heads and eyes down so as not to trip.

They passed few others as they traversed the streets. Those they did come upon stumbled through the fog like bloody specters, some masked and some nearly naked, their bodies covered with goosebumps. More often than not, they heard others before they saw them; disembodied laughter or more salacious sounds spilled from the fog ahead of them like ghosts. A few groups called to them, beckoning the two women to join in on a round of decadence and pleasure. E'lisea squeezed Niscene's hand as they passed, ignoring the invitations.

Finally, Niscene and the queen stopped at the street corner, beneath the dim lantern where they first met earlier that night. Still holding Niscene's hand, E'lisea turned to face her. "I hate to leave you," she said. She sighed like a lover leaving after a long-awaited tryst. "After such a night as this, how could I feel otherwise?" She sighed once more, then gazed at Niscene with eyes full of melancholy.

Niscene did not know what to say to any of this.

What kind of fool was this queen? Niscene had beaten her to within a bloody half-breath of her life and now the woman lamented their parting like some lovestruck maiden.

The queen smiled a wistful smile. "If gods be good," she said, "you shall haunt my dreams." Then, she raised a hand to Niscene's face, cupping her left cheek, and leaned in for a kiss. It was soft and sweet, tender and full of longing – unlike any kiss Niscene had ever known. She wanted to pull away but found she could not. Not at first. Again, she could not breathe; and her heart pounded as if it threatened to break forth from her chest. The same strange sensation from earlier once more swelled within her. *What is happening to me?* Suddenly, Niscene recoiled, nearly falling down into the cobbled street.

"You are a strange one," said the queen, with a sigh. "Powerful in magik and skilled in the painful pleasures, yet you bristle at a simple kiss." She tilted her head to the side, blue eyes regarding Niscene through the slits in her mask. "Most people don't mind my kiss."

"I am not most people," said Niscene, regaining some of her composure.

"That you are not," the queen agreed. "That you are

not." She pulled her shawl around her shoulders. "Well, good night, mistress," she said. She reached a hand out to stroke Niscene's cheek but she pulled away. The queen frowned then lowered her hand. "You may not enjoy my touch," she said. "But I rather enjoyed yours."

Niscene said nothing.

"I shall return just after sunset," the queen said. "Perhaps you won't be so afraid of my touch then." She leaned in as if again to kiss Niscene but stopped just short. She smiled, then withdrew. "Until the red haze falls, mistress."

With one final lingering gaze, the queen stepped away from beneath the street lamp, evanescing into the thick crimson mist of the Midnight Court.

SIXTH

STILL STANDING BENEATH the dull light of the street lamp, Niscene brought her fingers to her red lips and winced. Sweet and soft, yet full of melancholy and longing, the queen's kiss lingered like a memory she tried to forget.

Niscene E'terrall did not care for kissing. A lifetime of being forced to kiss men – with their rough, raw lips ripe with drink and harsh words – had left her with a bad taste for it. The last time she kissed a man, he left her with two black eyes and a bleeding cunt. Her hands twitched at her sides, balling into fists. The Sense hummed its vicious melody while the memory swirled inside of her. Oh, how she wished she could have made the bastard burn.

But the queen's kiss had been different. Unlike the kisses of men that held no emotion or kindness, E'lisea's kiss overflowed with passion and desire, tenderness and longing. Niscene felt her heart beat a little faster as she recalled that the queen's lips were soft as velvet and tasted not of drink, but were sweet, like honeysuckle on a warm spring day.

Something stirred deep inside of Niscene then. A kind of ache. An anticipation heretofore alien to her. The queen's parting words echoed in her ears, deepening the strange stirring inside of her: *"I hate to leave you."* Niscene took a deep breath and licked her lips. Yes. The queen's kiss was different.

Drawing out of her reverie, Niscene rubbed her eyes, and yawned. She glanced toward the east. Obscured by the dense red fog of the Midnight Court, the moon, still days from being full, hung low in the sky, its pale white light fading. Dawn was near and it was time for sleep.

She found quarter in an inn not far from where she met the queen. The Pleasure's Respite was known to board mistresses, whores, pillow friends, and others who flooded the capital to work the Midnight Court. A nondescript brick building, the three-story inn stood just on the boundary between the Midnight Court and the rest of Ramodin. The sign above the door creaked softly as Niscene entered. Almost immediately, she was greeted by a woman with sharp features and dark braided hair.

"Y'poor dear," the woman said in a greeting muddied by an accent of slurred words. "Y'look a'tho y'eve *seen* things." What things, she did not specify, instead regarding Niscene with a shrewd look, carefully eyeing her up and down. Then the sharp-featured woman circled her slowly, muttering to herself occasionally until the two women were again face to face.

"No bruises," said the woman, more to herself than Niscene. "'Le'st, no new'ins." Then she reached out to take Niscene's chin between her fingers. She scowled and tried to object but the braided woman clucked her into silence. She then made a *tsk-tsk* sound. "'Pologies, dear, 'pologies," she said as she moved Niscene's head back and forth by way of her chin. She stared hard and long into Niscene's onyx eyes, saying not a word until she nodded and dropped her beefy hand. "Yes, yes. Y'pain's in y'er eyes. Y'eve def'inly *seen* things." She clucked her tongue again and shook her head. Then she clapped her hands and turned, gesturing for Niscene to follow her. "Come, come!"

The woman led Niscene into the inn's common room, which was as nondescript as the inn's exterior. A few lamps dotted the room giving a subdued light. A dozen or so tables with varying numbers of chairs and benches were scattered about. A few sets of eyes glanced up to see the newcomer before quickly looking away, returning to their own tables and troubles. The room was eerily quiet, as though everyone were afraid to speak or simply preferred the silence to conversation. Niscene did not mind. She had enough to think on without having to listen to the troubles and sorrows of strangers.

The braided woman led Niscene to a vacant table and ushered her to sit. She then snapped her fingers and a serving girl suddenly appeared to set a steaming bowl in front of Niscene.

"Thank ye, dear," the sharp-featured woman said to the serving girl, who curtsied and scurried back from wherever she came.

Turning back to Niscene, the big woman said, "E't up, dear. E't up." She frowned and shook her head again. "Y'poor dear," she said. "Y'eve seen things. Yer eyes hide nothin' from ol' Eldra." Again, what things Niscene's eyes failed to hide, this Eldra did not specify, but a quick glance around gave Niscene an idea of what the woman meant.

Whores, mistresses, and pillow friends sat hunched over at the other tables. A few glanced up occasionally but most sat in silence, eyes downcast. Most were women – but Niscene noted a man or two who stuck to the corners like pariahs – their own meagre clothes hanging off their bodies. Some women wore nothing but what amounted to rags, which they held in place with weak hands to cover their breasts and sex. All present wore haunted expressions, their eyes hollow, contemplating in their hearts what they had seen and done. Niscene stifled a derisive snort. *Fool whores.*

"You e't up, girl," said Eldra, tapping the tabletop twice to regain Niscene's attention. "Then I'll show ye t' yer room. First night's free, 'o course."

Niscene nodded a feigned thanks and Eldra let her be. She scrutinized the bowl in front of her. Its contents appeared to be some kind of stew of beef with chopped carrots and possibly some other ingredients Niscene could not place. A growling sound came from her belly and she remembered how long it had been since she last ate. Niscene scooped a few spoonfuls of stew into her mouth then again scanned the room at the pathetic figures who wallowed at their tables. "Fool whores," she said softly, bringing another spoonful of stew to her lips.

At worst, the others in the room had been raped on the streets of the Midnight Court by overzealous patrons emboldened by the anonymity their black masks afforded them. Doubtless, some willingly gave themselves to men or women in exchange for some semblance of pleasure and a few meagre coins. But were any haunted by their patron's kiss? *"I hate to leave you."*

Again, that anomalous sensation struck Niscene somewhere deep inside, a curious ache of longing pushed from within her, threatening to burst forth. Niscene closed her eyes and saw E'lisea smiling at her. The queen leaned in and whispered, *"If gods be good, you shall haunt my dreams."*

A *tsk-tsk* sound drew Niscene from her thoughts. She opened her eyes to find Eldra beside her with a sympathetic frown on her sharp-featured face. "Poor dear, y'poor dear," the big woman said, shaking her head. "Leave 'im ye must. Don'a be fallin' in love now. It's the Mi'night Court – not a romance."

Niscene's face darkened. "Mind your tongue, woman," she hissed, seizing the Sense in an instant. "I am not—"

"'O course, 'o course," the woman, Eldra, said in her thick accent. She brushed away Niscene's reaction with a wave of her thick hand. "Y'say so, y'say so, dear." Eldra's lips twisted into a sympathetic smile before she scooped up the stew bowl and walked away.

Niscene's chair scraped against the wood floor as she stood, jaw clenched and onyx eyes staring daggers at the woman's back as she walked away. The Sense filled her.

Romance? What a foolish thought! At her sides, Niscene's fingers twitched as dozens of spells and incantations ran through her mind. The Sense pulsed through her, stoking her anger while also providing its sweet succor. Then the words again echoed through her mind: *"I hate to leave you."*

Even with the Sense's melody playing in her ears,

encouraging her to lash out with her power, Niscene stayed her hand. She licked her lips. Behind the more recent taste of beef and broth was the faint hint of honeysuckle in early spring. *"Until the red haze falls."* She raised a hand to wipe her lips.

"I'll show ye t' yer room now," said Eldra, whose reappearance gave Niscene a start. The large woman offered a sympathetic smile. "'Pologies, dear. Din't mean t' frighten ye. Come a'long now, dear. This way, this way."

Gesturing for Niscene to follow, Eldra turned to leave the common room. Niscene clenched her jaw, doing her best to keep her bubbling anger at bay. The Sense howled, pushing her to teach the woman a lesson. *She's just a fool*, Niscene reassured herself. *Let her think what she will. I know what I must do.*

Bracing herself, Niscene let go of the Sense. It evaporated like desert water. Despite her preparation, though, she still felt the sudden jolt of loss. When she held the Sense Niscene felt alive with sharpened senses and physical abilities – and the magik, of course – that when she let it go it was like waking from a dream, leaving her dazed and empty.

Eldra had waited for her by the stairs in the main foyer of the inn. The innkeeper led Niscene up three flights of aged stairs to a room at the end of the third floor hall. The woman pulled a ring of keys from somewhere and inserted one into the lock. After a small click, she pushed open the door then handed the key to Niscene.

"As I said, first night's free," Eldra said. "Two c'pper each night after."

Niscene nodded as she walked into the small room. Like the room where she had spent the past few hours, it wasn't much. A tired-looking chair in the back corner and a small oak wardrobe in another. A lone beam of moonlight shone through the window. In the middle of everything was a simple bed with a lumpy mattress.

When she caught sight of the bed, Niscene's eyelids became heavy. She yawned. Likely, Eldra bid her good night and closed the door as she left. If she did, Niscene did not hear any of it. Exhaustion had finally won out, casting out thoughts of all else save sleep. The Sense began to hum a soothing, restful melody, almost like a lullaby and Niscene sighed.

Without word or thought, she fumbled her way to the

bed and collapsed into sleep.

Niscene E'terrall never dreamed. When she slept, the world stopped, went utterly silent, allowing a respite from the chaotic nightmare of her life. But that night, in the inn on the outskirts of the Midnight Court, the woman who never dreamed, dreamt. Having lived a lifetime of dreamless slumber, she was unaware of what they were, the scenes and shadows that danced and played out before her, taking shape and form.

She was a little girl again, her auburn hair in two braids on either side of her head. Dolls in her hands, she moved them up and down on the floor and mouthed words in silly voices for each. She smiled and giggled as she played. Though she knew she was a little girl, something scratched at the back of her mind. A notion or feeling or sense that something was wrong – that she was not a little girl, that this was but a shadow of a time long past. She ignored it.

A door creaked opened behind her and young Niscene heard footsteps approach. Her hands paused in mid-play, the dolls staring at each other with their vacant button eyes. Niscene raised her head to see who stood behind her.

He wore the same grin he always did: the left side of his mouth twisted upward, open just enough to reveal a hint of perfectly white teeth. The older girls and ladies all across the city called him handsome. But that pretty face was but a mask, hiding a monstrous visage. "Playtime's over, Niscene," he said. A restrained viciousness flashed in his hazel eyes.

Niscene trembled as she stared up at her brother, Login. She heard more footsteps, then the sound of nasty, wet laughter. Login's friends had arrived. Niscene's breath caught in her young throat and she began to panic. Tears threatened and finally broke through; they streaked down her cheeks and she whimpered, clutching her dolls close. "Please," she whispered through her tears. She stared up at her brother, her onyx eyes wide and pleading. "Login, please," she said. "No mor–"

Niscene's vision suddenly flashed white then burst into a rainbow of colors. A bloom of pain throbbed on her cheeks. She blinked and realized she was on the ground, crying. Her eyes found her brother, who was rubbing his right hand with his left. "'No' is not an option, Niscene," he said. "Remember."

Weeping uncontrollably now, Niscene managed to nod. The two bigger boys flanking Login moved in then. One grabbed her arm and pulled her up violently causing her to cry out as her shoulder nearly dislocated. He then slipped a hand beneath her skirt and she wept. The other boy began to undo his breeches. Niscene closed her eyes and prayed to the Maker for mercy and eventually to any god that might listen. None did.

When she opened her eyes again, Niscene was awake, warm and sweaty. Breathing heavily, she stared at the ceiling of her room in the Pleasure's Respite. Her heart pounded in her ears and she took a deep breath to calm herself. She soon sat up in bed and rubbed her temples. Her body shook, trembling with the vividness of the dream. It had felt so real, as if she truly were reliving the horror her brother and his lecherous friends had set upon her. Years such torture lasted. Niscene spent her adolescence living in fear of Login and his degenerate friends. Until she seized the Sense. Until she made them burn.

The Sense stirred at the fringes of her mind. Without

hesitation, she reached out and seized it. Its power and magik flooded into her and Niscene sighed, content, comforted. Her heartbeat slowed. The Sense sang its dark melody.

Eventually, she found a dreamless sleep.

SEVENTH

NISCENE E'TERRALL WOKE late and ate little of what was offered in the common room. Save a brief interaction with Eldra to pay for the next night, she spoke to no one, and no one tried to speak to her. Patrons of the Pleasure's Respite were a veritable sorority of silence. The whores and pleasure mistresses and pillow friends all shared experiences and the same hollow-eyed expression but kept their distance from each other as best they could, and saying nothing. Such an environment served Niscene well.

She spent the afternoon hours in her room, with the curtains pulled tight to block any sunlight, shrouding her in darkness and shadow. For years, of course, they had birthed a fear in her. Now they provided a strange comfort. She listened to the Sense sing its terrible, haunting song.

For much of the day, she dwelled on her dream. Never before had her slumbering mind conjured memories or visions. Sleep was her respite, her escape. From where had it come? What did it mean? Her brother, Login, and his half-smile, the same expression he wore every time he watched a man fuck her. Again she was a scared little girl, burning and bleeding between her legs. A wave of shame rose up in her, only to be smothered by a white-hot anger. *Where are you, brother?* His lecherous friends had burned, but somehow Login had vanished. In the darkness of her room, Niscene threw back her head and let loose a violent scream.

When her voice went hoarse and tears threatened behind her eyes, she seized the Sense for comfort just as she had when seeking sleep. Its tempestuous, chaotic power soothed her. Login was still out there, somewhere in the world. "I will find you, brother," she vowed to the shadows. Pulsing within her, the Sense hummed its sweet, horrible melody.

Then, there was the queen. E'lisea. The woman

sentenced to die by Ash'an Rah and Death Herself. *"If gods be good, you shall haunt my dreams."* The woman's words made Niscene shudder. If only the moon were full.

By the time the sun set and the moon rose high, Niscene E'terrall was on edge, ready to lash out, to kill. Walking through the Midnight Court, with degenerates and debauchery at every turn, did nothing to sate her anguish. Two men wearing nothing but black masks and loincloths followed her a ways, grabbing at her, teasing and begging for her to join them for the night – until her frustration boiled over and she seized the Sense and removed their fingernails. Their screams were piercing enough to curdle blood. Music to Niscene's ears.

Soon, she turned down the familiar street and her eyes found the queen, standing at ease beneath the lamp. Her strawberry blonde curls were styled in a swirl above her head. She wore a dark, possibly black, sleeveless gown that emphasized her bosom. It hugged the woman's hips before flaring out at the calves. A dark, sheer shawl clung to her shoulders. Upon seeing the queen, the tension that had built up most of the day evanesced and Niscene's lips twitched upward into a smile.

The queen turned her head. "There you are," she said as Niscene stopped beside her. "I thought the sun would never set."

E'lisea then grabbed Niscene's hand, bowed, and kissed it to lay claim to her mistress for the evening. The touch of the other woman's soft velvet lips against her skin sent a pleasant jolt through Niscene's body. Her smile widened.

"My mistress is in a pleasant mood, it seems," said E'lisea, more than a hint of mirth in her voice. From behind her black mask, her blue eyes regarded Niscene, and flickered.

"Oh, yes," Niscene said in a sultry whisper. "I am." And she was, but knew not why. Along the edges of her mind, the Sense sang to her, as it always did; but something else, something strange and sweet and new, also reached out to her. Meeting the queen's eyes, she felt her heartbeat quicken. Was her breath growing short, as well? She swallowed hard and took a deep breath. Then, with a gentle touch, she pushed aside a loose strand of the queen's blonde hair. E'lisea shuddered and Niscene inched closer.

The rest of the Midnight Court vanished from her mind. All she saw, all she knew, was the queen.

"I dreamt of you," said E'lisea. Her breath was warm against Niscene's face.

"And I, you," Niscene lied, wishing it had been so. The realization made her shiver, or perhaps it was the early spring chill in the air. Suddenly, that strange sweetness swelled inside of her, overwhelming her like ocean waves. Without second thought or preamble, Niscene kissed the queen. E'lisea's lips trembled briefly, then she wrapped a hand around Niscene's waist and drew her closer, returning the kiss with fervor and desire. Niscene's eyes fluttered and she melted into the other woman's embrace and her sweet, velvet lips that tasted of honeysuckle and springtime.

Niscene's entire body buzzed and hummed, a thousand wonderful sensations erupting at once. The rest of the world disappeared. Even the Sense, which called to her, as always, was forgotten in that moment. To Niscene, there was only herself and the queen, kissing passionately amid the crimson haze of the Midnight Court. Her heart pounded faster and a hunger awoke within her. Desires she never knew before filled her mind and heart and loins. She pulled the queen closer.

E'lisea pulled away first and it was jarring. Niscene barely stifled a whimper. The sudden loss was much like when she let go of the Sense. When the queen stroked her cheek, Niscene closed her eyes and breathed in the woman's scent.

"I knew you'd come around," said E'lisea, her lips widening into a salacious smile. Even through the red haze of the Midnight Court, her blue eyes flashed with satisfaction. "Come," she commanded. The queen slipped her hand into Niscene's then gave a gentle squeeze. "Our room awaits."

Soon, the two women again found themselves in the dimly lit upstairs room, with the creaky wooden floorboards and round bed, over which the metal restraints swayed back and forth. Niscene's nose wrinkled when they entered; the scent of stale sweat, old blood, and other unseemly odors clung to the room. The queen stood beneath the bed, gazing up at her fetters, anticipation flashing in her eyes.

Despite the environs, Niscene felt an overpowering desire to kiss the queen again. The Sense made a strange sound but she ignored it, eyes locked on E'lisea. Certain thoughts once more flooded her mind as she looked the woman up and down with something like a hunger. Over her shoulder, the queen noticed and pursed her lips.

"Two men begged me to spend the night with them," she said. With a crooked finger, she gestured for Niscene to come closer then offered her back. "They were quite insistent. But I was, as well." She laughed at some secret joke.

Niscene brought up her hands to begin undoing the queen's gown. A flash of jealousy roared within her. "I'd have sliced off their balls and left them to bleed out on the cobblestones," she said. If the queen reacted to her words, she paid it no mind. She breathed in the woman's sweet scent as she slowly undressed her. "I've done it before."

And she had. Her lips twitched into a smile at the memory: the echo of some lordling's piercing scream as she sliced off his balls from between his legs. How she relished that scream. Until he tried to retaliate. Then she slit the fool's throat.

"Truly?" asked the queen, cocking her head. "You've *truly* cut off some poor man's balls?" Her tone betrayed the intent of her question. She did not doubt it.

"Aye," Niscene whispered into the woman's ear. She nibbled softly on it, drawing a moan and tremor from her majesty. She untied the final knot.

"How vicious of you," E'lisea said, with a shudder. She turned to face Niscene and allowed the front of her gown to fall, revealing her milk-white breasts and flawless body, which seemed to glow in the darkness of the stale room.

Niscene's eyes took in the queen's chest. Her heartbeat quickened even more and a thousand ideas of what she might do to the woman raced through her mind. "He deserved it." She raised her eyes. "All men do."

"All men," the queen repeated, slightly amused. A smile tugged at her lips. How Niscene wished again to kiss them, so full and red and soft, tasting of springtime and honeysuckle. She licked her own lips, expectantly, then received her wish.

The queen's body pressed against Niscene, firm yet gentle. Much to Niscene's surprise, the closeness, the touch, excited her almost as much as the kissing. The kiss was soft, of course, and tender; but also demure, submissive, longing. And when the queen pulled away again and spoke, Niscene knew why.

"What do I deserve?" the queen asked pathetically.

Niscene's face darkened, then she seized the Sense, its sweet darkness soaking into her being. With a gesture, she slapped the shackles around the queen's wrists and hoisted her into the air with a look.

A breath later, the queen began to scream.

The queen cried out. "Oh, gods! More! Yes! *Gods!*"

The Sense pulsing through her, Niscene unleashed blow after blow against the woman. E'lisea huffed and howled and screamed with a ferocious pleasure. Each hit erupted against her, sending her body into convulsions and twists and contortions. Niscene could not help but shudder herself. Bringing pain to the woman evoked a pleasure of her own. Streaks of dark blood lined the queen's body, chest and back, arms and legs; bruises and welts swelled on her legs and even her face. How sweet it was, delivering pain to this woman, this queen with the soft, red lips and longing in her voice. *"I thought the sun would never set."*

Amid the swirling of the Sense and other sensations within her, Niscene felt warm. Her body grew hotter, as if she were being swallowed by a dragon. All of a sudden, the Sense winced within her, jolted by some unknown force. Hotter and hotter Niscene became, beads of sweat streaking down her face.

She let loose another blow. The queen screamed. Nearly feverish, Niscene wiped at her brow. She blinked and cried out, causing her to lose her grip on the Sense; Niscene winced at the sudden emptiness and fell to her hands and knees on the hard wooden floor. Her body was on fire.

Her knees began to throb and her wrists ached from her collapse. Above her, the queen breathed heavily, her chains clinking softly. The Sense was silent.

"Mistress?" the queen mumbled. "What…what happened?"

Niscene pressed her forehead to the floor, attempting to cool down. *So warm.* Instinctually, she reached for the Sense, but something was wrong. The ever-present melody had vanished. She could not hear the Sense. The realization pushed her into a panic. Reaching out again she searched for it, clawed for it. "Where are *you*?" she hissed. "Please – come back! I can't–"

"Mistress? What's wrong?" asked the queen, her voice raw but growing more concerned.

Niscene moaned and pounded her aching hands softly on the floor. "The Sense..." she bemoaned. "I cannot find it!" A burning sensation that started in her chest moved up into her throat then behind her eyes until finally tears burst through. Bitter and salty, they stung as they fell down her cheeks. Niscene shook and shivered, contemplating the void, the emptiness that threatened to overwhelm her. What had happened? Where was the Sense? Her ever-present dark passenger, constantly calling to her from the edge of consciousness, was gone.

Soon, the emotion of her personal loss was overcome by a far more fearful thought: Ash'an Rah. Without the Sense, how could she hope to accomplish her assignment? Weak and alone without the power the Sense provided, Niscene was as good as dead. "Maker's mercy!" she murmured.

"The Sense is not lost," said a voice in her ear followed by the warm embrace of arms wrapping around her shoulders. It was the queen. Somehow she had managed to free herself from her shackles. "It is never lost.

You control the Sense. But you must embrace it like a lover." Her voice was weak from screaming and her body was sticky with blood. Still, Niscene had wallowed in worse; and she found the woman's presence a strange comfort, even if her words stung and confused. She had never controlled the Sense. It was not part of her, nor hers to wield unless it allowed; since the day she first heard its seductive song, the Sense teased and tempted of its own will.

Feebly, she reached out to the penumbra of her mind to seize the Sense; but she found nothing. Numbness came over her. Stifling a whimper, Niscene whispered, "You're wrong."

"I'll show you," the queen said. Then, just as a fresh wave of tears threatened, Niscene discerned the tiniest sensation on the back of her neck. Small, wet kisses made their way up and down her neck, while fingertips gently caressed her auburn hair. Lifting her head, Niscene turned to look at the queen, whose face remained unhealed. A deep cut dissected her left cheek and her velvet lips were puffy and bloody. Despite her appearance, the woman's blue eyes possessed an intense concern and tenderness, entirely directed at Niscene.

"I do not deserve..." she said, but failed to finish. Even bloody, even inflamed, the queen's lips drew her closer until she kissed them, letting loose a long-dormant passion, a desire that flared to life as if it had waited for this exact moment. The queen responded in kind, meeting the potency of Niscene's passion with her own.

On the floor, the two women maneuvered and adjusted until they were a mess of interlocking limbs sliding up and down along raw, wet skin. In the heat of their embrace, the queen parted her lips just so and her tongue tentatively pushed its way into Niscene's mouth, gently caressing its counterpart. Niscene pulled the queen closer, their bodies taut against each other, as her tongue responded, falling into a manic, eager dance with the queen's. They exchanged soft moans, losing themselves to the moment.

Guided by her unleashed desire, Niscene's hands slid up and down the queen's bloody and bruised body, eliciting short convulsions of pleasure from the other woman.

"Oh, gods, yes!" the queen gasped when Niscene's hands brushed the sex between her legs. Soon, both sets of hands found their way to places and regions of each body heretofore untouched. Niscene's whole body tingled when the queen's hands caressed her midsection and moved upward, slipping into her bodice to cup her breasts. The queen began untying the piece of clothing and Niscene nearly screamed.

Yes, thought Niscene, feeling her consciousness, her very being, on the precipice of a tall cliff, about to free-fall into the moment before her – a moment she never imagined she would be a part of. With each touch, her body quivered. With each kiss, her mind hummed. She had come to kill this woman but without her Sense, she now gave herself to her. With her Sense gone, Niscene's assignment – and therefore, her very life – was forfeit. In time, Ash'an Rah would find her, do with her what he will. Kill her, torture her, burn her alive; it mattered little to her now, on the floor with the queen, whose touch and taste evoked such desire and sensation. She was in the Midnight Court with the queen of the Unified Kingdom, kissing and touching like she never had any man, her mind and heart exploding with new ideas and thoughts and desires.

Then, she heard. Somewhere far off on the fringes of

consciousness, yet so close Niscene swore she could touch it if she wished, came a melody, both familiar and new. Between the kisses and sensations and her newfound sexual desire, the song played, humming and growing with each moan, each impassioned plea for more. Haunting and beautiful, it grew louder, an aria calling to her from across the void between the conscious and the unconscious. With each shudder of her body, with each tingle of her skin, with each new luscious taste, the music grew louder and louder still, until it nearly was on top of her, nearly engulfing her.

Between the near-deafening melody and tingling of her body, Niscene was awash in a powerful swirl of desire and pleasure. The pressure of both mounted, mounted, mounted until it crescendoed in a crashing wave of release and relief. On the floor, Niscene arched her back, thrusting forward, stealing every hint of pleasure and satisfaction until she fell back against the wooden floorboards; her body stopped but her mind continued to fall backward, ever closer to the still-sounding song of beautiful harmonious magik. At the final moment, she sighed in relief, just as she embraced it.

"Oh, gods…" she whispered as she lay on the floor,

half naked, staring at the shadows on the ceiling.

The Sense flooded into her, then, filling every pore, every corner of her being. That familiar magik and power pulsed through her. The sweetness! So, so sweet was the Sense, like a long-lost lover come home. She relished in its return, seizing it, clinging to it, cradling it, steeling her grip. She marveled at subtle changes suddenly realized. No longer was it a nearly unwieldy torrent of chaos in her mind; rather, Niscene possessed greater control over it than ever before.

At Niscene's midriff, the queen raised her head. "As lover embraces lover, so shall you embrace the Sense." Her lips then widened into a coquettish grin. "You were better than in my dreams."

EIGHTH

NISCENE BARELY REGISTERED the woman's words. The
Sense had returned and she lay on the floor, half naked,
relishing its dulcet tones and sweet comfort. She let out an
extended moan while running her hands down her face,
then stretched like a cat, eliciting a laugh from the queen.
Almost without a thought, Niscene rapped a whip of air
across the other woman's bare bottom. The sudden smack
evoked a tiny, surprised gasp.

"Paeter," said the queen, her blue eyes flickering with
amusement from behind her leather mask. She pulled
herself off the floor. Turning her back, she reached for the

ceiling in a long, languid stretch. Niscene sat up and regarded her with keen eyes. E'lisea was still marked by innumerable lashes; dry blood had begun to crust in some places. The queen glanced over her shoulder and winked. Her honeysuckle lips were still inflamed and puffy. A brief flash of blue-green light enveloped the woman, and, mere moments later, her body stitched itself together: bruises and cuts vanished, the swelling in her lips was gone.

The woman again stretched toward the ceiling then bent her body toward the floor. "Healing is its own sort of pleasure," she said, standing. With a soft murmuring moan, she ran her hands over her naked body. While the physical markings of her beating were gone, dry and crusty bits of blood remained. "Shall we wash?" she asked, extending her hand to lift up Niscene.

How she wished she could have lain there weaving and casting and enchanting her magik while watching this queen who had awakened some deep, unknown desire within her. When Niscene took E'lisea's hand that familiar tingle shot through her body. *Must I kill you, my queen?*

The night air was warm and the red haze of the Midnight

Court hung low as the women ventured into the streets. As before, the haze had thickened into a heavy fog that made it difficult to see. Disembodied hoots and howls raced and echoed around the two women. They were finished earlier than the previous night, meaning more patrons and purveyors of pleasure remained in the midst of their debaucheries and desires. The queen laughed at one particularly husky sound that emanated from somewhere above.

"My husband makes that same sound after much drink when he demands his due," she said. She imitated the gruff, husky moan, deepening as best she could her own high-pitched voice. The imitation was so foolish, Niscene could not help but laugh. The queen squeezed her hand, sending a fresh tingling jolt through Niscene. "Thank the gods, he spends himself rather quickly," she continued. "However, he then falls into such a dreadful fit of snoring I sneak away to another bed so I might sleep."

As the women turned down the next street, they heard the sound of boots on stone and the grumbling of men somewhere close by.

"—can't see a bloody thing in this fog!" cried a gruff

voice. "Well, who's that there?"

Just then, three men pushed through the crimson murk right in front of the women. They wore brown coats, though the Midnight Court's red hue warped the color. Niscene lifted her head and met the gaze of the lead man. His wide forehead furrowed and a slimy grin stretched across his lined face.

"Hello, pretty, pretty," he said. He whistled at the women. "Come closer and let us see that pretty face of yours. The night is still young and we've coin enough for two."

In its song, the Sense hit a harsh note, mirroring the annoyance that shot through Niscene. She met the man's deep-set eyes but made no response as she and the queen walked past him and his fellows.

"Come, come!" the man cried after them. "Lift your skirt and I'll say hello!" He followed his words with a strange guttural sound that evoked laughter from his comrades.

"Men always think we can't live without their cocks," whispered the queen. Niscene's ensuing laugh echoed through the heavy red fog.

Soon thereafter, the women reached their street corner. The street lamp was a dull solitary dot of light that barely broke through the fog even while they stood beneath it.

"Our time together passes far too quickly," said the queen. "The Philosophers say it is a sin to wish away one's days." E'lisea reached up to cup Niscene's face, then kissed her. Niscene inhaled the scent of honeysuckle and springtime. She wrapped her hands around the queen, bringing her closer. She lost hold of the Sense but barely noticed its absence as she sought to lose herself in the queen's embrace.

"I hate to leave you," the queen whispered.

"And I, you," Niscene responded, and knew it for true. Alarmed, she suddenly lost her voice. She stepped back and looked at her hands, as though they possessed answers to the questions that suddenly rushed through her mind. She opened her mouth then closed it when no words came.

The queen placed a hand over her mouth, stifling a laugh. "Good night, mistress," she said, delight and a hint of mischief flashing in her eyes. "I shall see you in my dreams." She leaned in for one final, lingering kiss that still ended far too soon, then stepped out into the street vanishing like a ghost in the red mist.

Niscene let out a shudder; goosebumps popped up all over her body. *What have you done to me, woman?* At the edge of consciousness, the Sense stirred, calling to her in its familiar melody, a chaotic, staccato aria. Then, the song suddenly ceased, and a vision of a dark, hooded figure flashed across her mind. Two slits of red gazed out from within the dark hood. Ash'an Rah. "I am a Servant of the Lady of Death," Niscene said in a hushed voice. She recited the Oath like a creed.

Harsh laughter broke off her catechism. Momentarily shaken, Niscene threw a quick glance over her shoulder; anonymous figures moved along the street, shrouded in the Midnight Court's ever-present red haze. She shivered then silently cursed herself for being foolish. Without another thought, she reached out to seize the Sense – but could not grab it!

"Pretty, pretty," came a voice she recognized. "All alone in the night. Where's your friend?" Familiar laugher echoed behind Niscene. Again, she reached for the Sense –

which she saw floating along the penumbra of her mind, calling to her as always – but could not seize it. The frigid breath of fear then whispered on her neck. She ran.

"After her!" the lead man cried.

Running through the crimson fog, Niscene was blind. She desperately lashed out for the Sense but could not grab it. She knew it was there, calling to her with its soft melody – but why could she not wield it? *Gods, no! You're right there! I feel you! I see you!* The Sense swirled, just out of reach. Desperate, Niscene called out for help.

"We hear you, bitch!" a man growled behind her.

Without a thought, she turned, thinking she had reached the end of the street. Seconds later, her head and body struck cold stone and she collapsed to the ground. A sharp pang blossomed all over her body, and she groaned softly, barely holding onto consciousness. Boots scraped on the dirt of the alley behind her. Fighting the throb in her body and sudden dizziness in her head, Niscene managed to pick herself up. She licked her lips and tasted blood.

Out of the red fog, a meaty hand appeared, grabbing at Niscene's hair and pulling hard. She screamed. In desperation, she scratched at the opaque fog but two other hands appeared and stopped her. She felt her arms being twisted behind her and she cried out in pain. "Maker's mercy!" she screamed.

"Oh, the Maker is anything but merciful," said a rough voice. "Looks like he abandoned you long ago." The rest laughed. Through the fog, three sinister faces appeared, twisted, hungry expressions staring at her. Niscene squeezed her eyes shut as she was thrown to the ground. At the edge of awareness, she saw the Sense. She stretched for it but its proximity was a tease.

"Why?" Niscene cried out. "Oh, gods, why?"

Suddenly, Niscene felt herself being turned over onto her stomach. Her chin slammed hard on the ground, breaking it open. Heavy weight pressed on her legs and arms and back, squeezing out what little air was left in her lungs. She felt clammy hands slide down the sides of her body and then move over and smack her bottom. Those same hands continued down farther, forcing apart her legs. "No, please," Niscene cried frantically. "Login, please! No! No!" Suddenly, her brother's vicious face flashed in her mind. *"No' is not an option, Niscene."*

She heard her skirt rip away and the chill of the heavy

fog make contact with her exposed skin. A hand caressed her bottom then gave it another hard smack. Niscene yelped, eliciting more laughter from the men. "Oh, pretty, pretty," said the lead man. "It's going to hurt much, much more."

Slowly, Niscene's world went numb; the pain all over her body, the cut on her chin, the clammy hands groping – all sensation and feeling vanished, leaving her alone, the Sense hovering just out of reach on the fringes of her mind. How had it come to this – men holding her down, forcing themselves upon her? She had vowed it never would happen again. Never. Again.

Niscene wanted to scream. She wanted to lash out with fire and death and chaos, to grab hold of and unleash the power that called to her, unceasing. But she could not. She clawed at the fringes of her mind to seize the Sense, but it remained elusive, as though it pulled away the closer she came to it. Strangely, it now howled and raged, seething like an angry god; its melody was a discordant mess of wrath and fury.

Niscene gasped as a hand slid between her legs. "Time to say hello," said the man on top of her. His fellows laughed and laughed and laughed.

Suddenly, the Sense roared, erupting like a tempest across the void from where it stirred. In a fiery mania, the Sense thrummed and clapped like thunder; it reverberated like a plucked harp string, sending a violent shudder through Niscene's mind. All around her, she heard a piercing melody, terrible and great, like a banshee in the night. Louder and louder it became, overwhelming her until she thought her ears would burst and her mind would melt.

"Make it stop!" she cried. She could not hear herself. "Oh, gods, make it stop!"

In agony, she desperately pulled at her arms, struggling against the weight of her attackers. To her surprise, her hands came free and she clasped them to her ears to block out the deafening song. A moment later, her head snapped back and she let out a scream as the Sense shot into her like a bolt of lightning, its sweet song of anger and rage roiling and crashing throughout her being.

Despite the shock of it all, Niscene clung to it, to the sweet Sense, seizing the power that had been out of reach. Her eyes shot open and, as if guided by some unseen force, rose to her feet.

All around her was a blur of red fog and blue lightning and fearful faces and sinister laughter. And the Sense. Oh, the Sense! Full of fury and anger and rage and chaos, its song was all she heard, all she knew, all she wanted. It nearly deafened her, but she did not care.

Niscene was on her feet, manipulating and using the Sense in strange, powerful new ways. Her lips muttered new spells and incantations as flashes of green light emitted from her fingertips; bolts of blue momentarily lit up the alley. Men screamed but she laughed and laughed. Men shouted and wept. Niscene feasted on their cries and the power she wielded.

Questions scratched at the back of her mind but the Sense dulled them with its reverberating thrum; its song was unlike any she had heard. Sinister yet playful. Threatening yet sweet. A melody borne of chaos and darkness but also of form and beauty, like something out of a dream.

"Please! No! No! Nooo!" The frightened shrieks of men filled the air, followed by the fumbling of feet and clattering of steel and boots slapping against the brick and cobblestone. And then, as suddenly as it had rushed into her, the Sense winked out and Niscene cried out in shock. The void threatened to come up and swallow her whole.

Disoriented, she stumbled about, blinded by the heavy crimson fog. She took a step and her legs buckled. She fell to her knees. She felt as if her heart had been ripped out of her chest. All she heard was a woman's threatening voice transform into mischievous laughter. Beside her, she thought she saw the the outline of a familiar figure. Time then slowed and her eyes rolled back into her head. Niscene crumpled to the cold ground and darkness was all she knew.

NINTH

WHEN NISCENE OPENED her eyes, she felt the pounding in her head immediately. It felt as if a blacksmith were hammering away at her. She could barely keep her eyes open. Above her, she made out a blurry face.

"She's a'wakin'," said a voice Niscene knew to be Eldra, the innkeeper of the Pleasure's Respite. Another indistinguishable face then entered her line of vision.

"Maker's mercy!" exclaimed another familiar voice. "Thank the gods."

Confused, and with a thousand questions flooding her hazy, pounding mind, Niscene opened her mouth to speak, but fell into a coughing fit that sent a jolt of pain throughout her entire body. When it subsided, she groaned. Her head throbbed. But she could manage to keep her eyes open.

Slowly, full awareness returned and Niscene realized she was lying in her bed at the Pleasure's Respite. How she had gotten there, she could not recall. Her mind was a mess of foggy memories that she tried to piece together, but the pounding in her head did not allow her to focus.

"What...happened?" she managed to ask. Her voice was creaky and raw, nearly like an old woman's. She tried to clear her throat, but that triggered a fresh fit of coughing and magnified the powerful ache in her head.

When she managed to cease her coughing, Niscene felt something cool press against her lips.

"Drink, dear," said Eldra, the innkeeper.

Her vision finally clearing up, Niscene noticed the hard-faced woman standing over her. Eldra's lips were turned down in a deep frown.

"Drink," the innkeeper repeated. Her voice was firmer.

Annoyance flashed inside Niscene, but she obeyed

nonetheless. When she opened her mouth, a thick, bitter liquid assaulted her tongue and proceeded down her throat. She nearly gagged on the strange brew, which drew a tongue clucking from Eldra.

When Niscene had emptied the cup, Eldra withdrew it and gave a sharp nod of her head. "That should do f'now."

Niscene's lips twitched as if still tasting the bitterness of the drink. But in spite of the lingering aftertaste, she noted that the hammering in her head had somewhat softened.

"What happened?" she asked again, fixing her eyes on the innkeeper. "I was...how did I get here?"

"I brought you here," came that familiar voice again. When E'lisea's face entered her line of sight, Niscene felt a surge of desire rush through her. Her heart beat faster, and she felt her lips twist into a smile. The queen, too, smiled, and her blue eyes flashed from behind her black leather mask.

"'Tis been a long few days," said the innkeeper. "I'll leave y'two be." Without another word, she turned and left.

Niscene heard a door open, allowing a small sliver of

light into the dark room. A moment later, it shut, taking away the light. She turned her attention back to the queen. "Days?" she asked.

"Yes, mistress," said E'lisea, running a gentle, cool hand across Niscene's forehead. "You've been asleep for two days now."

"*Two days?*" Niscene croaked, the shock of this news rekindling the powerful pounding in her head. "But that means…" Her heart nearly stopped and she trailed off. Niscene tried to gaze out the window – to find the moon. Had she missed it? Had the full moon passed?

"I'm afraid it is my fault," said E'lisea. "Those damnable bastards had you blocked from the Sense. There was no other way."

The queen's words broke Niscene's fearful reverie. Despite the ache in her head, she gave a start. "Blocked?" she asked.

"Yes," E'lisea said. "One of the men, he…was strong. I…" The queen's voice was shaky. "Please, mistress, I knew no other way to save you!"

Flashes of memory flickered across Niscene's mind. Of the men chasing her. Of the alley. Of how the Sense seemed to remain just out of reach as she clawed for it. *Of course!* What else would that have been but a block? How could she have been such a fool? Difficult to discern, blocks kept one separate from the Sense. Niscene had learned the hard way how debilitating blocks could be. Soon after escaping the whore house, she attempted to use the Sense to pick the pocket of a merchant on the streets of El'deral only to have a watchful Philosopher block her from doing so. She quickly learned to detect such tricks.

But when it came to that group of would-be rapers, she had failed. And it nearly cost her. Anger rose up within her but the flare of emotion only served to agitate her throbbing head.

She saw and heard the Sense, in its familiar place at the periphery of her consciousness. Out of habit – but cautiously – she reached out for the Sense, for its soothing succor. But as she seized it, her stomach twisted and her mind spun. Frightened and confused, Niscene retracted. A whimper escaped her lips. She shivered.

"You poor thing," the queen said, stroking Niscene's forehead. The woman's touch was cool. "Gods, you're burning up!" A second later, Niscene felt a familiar tingle spread over her forehead followed by a jolt of pleasant coolness. The pounding of her head softened to a dull throb, and Niscene heaved a sigh of relief.

But – if she had been blocked, then how did she end up in her room at the inn? How had she escaped her attackers? Niscene closed her eyes, trying to recall the scene, to piece together what happened. She remembered clawing for the Sense, remembered seeing it floating just out of reach on the fringes of her mind. She recalled the men's laughter, malevolent and cruel. She recalled how they held her down, the shriek of her ripping skirt and the ensuing goosebumps that dotted her exposed skin. The stinging smack against her bottom. *"It's going to hurt much, much more."*

But then? The Sense exploded in some strange, piercing melody before it flooded into her. Niscene focused on that moment, the familiar haunting sweetness of the Sense. But that was not all. No. There had been her Sense, yes, sinister and sweet; its chaotic melody rang in her ears, its dark magik worked through her. But there also had been something else. Something unfamiliar – yet eerily similar.

"Oh, mistress, I am sorry," said E'lisea. "The *Sei'na.* I

had no choice. Had I known…"

"The *what?*" Niscene's eyes shot open. Her throat felt like she had screamed bloody murder. She coughed violently, nearly vomiting.

"There, there," the queen soothed, stroking Niscene's auburn hair and wiping spittle from her lips. "Oh, mistress, I *am* sorry. The *Sei'na* was the only way to break through their block."

Again, that word. It sounded strange to Niscene's ears. She repeated it as best she could, like a question: "*Sei'na?*"

"The shared Sense," said the queen. "I'd only ever read about it. But seeing how strong the block was, I knew I had to try. I reached through you to embrace your Sense. I've never attempted it before. I only…there wasn't time to…it can leave one ill – or so I've read. I…" E'lisea's face fell into her hands and her whole body shuddered. "I fear that is what happened with you, mistress." She sighed deeply. "I'm so sorry," she whispered. "But it was the only way to save you."

Shared Sense? Niscene had never heard of such a thing. Was it possible? The thought of another wielding her magik twisted her insides. On the margins of her consciousness, the Sense stirred violently, angrily, at learning of such a violation. Niscene grimaced at its irritation, but she shared in its reaction. At her sides, she clenched her hands into fists. She felt the rage build inside. Her onyx eyes hardened.

"You used *my* Sense?" she hissed. She attempted to sit up but her head swirled and her stomach twisted into knots, which further fueled her agitation and anger. "Made me dance on strings like a puppet?" She sucked in a breath to say more but it caught in her throat and she began to cough violently.

E'lisea gasped at the accusation. "Mistress, no! Please, I'm sorry! Those men had you on the ground; they were going to..." Trailing off, she tried to comfort Niscene. "It was the only way to save you!"

"No!" growled Niscene pushing away the queen's hands. "Away with you! I never wish to see you again! Go! Be *gone!*" She lashed out with clenched fists. It proved difficult, coughing as she did, but she managed to connect with the queen's face. A moment later, Niscene's body shook so fiercely from her violent coughing that she fell from her bed. Ignoring the sudden pain wracking her body, she coughed into one hand while waving away any assistance with the other. "Be–" she hacked into her hand. "Gone – with you!" She fell into a relentless fit of coughing and hacking that made her body convulse and ache until her eyes watered. She reached for the Sense, hopeful its sweetness would offer relief, but her body shook so violently she could not focus well enough to seize it.

Soon enough, her spasms ceased and Niscene lay prostrate on the floor gulping down tiny breaths. Her body throbbed as she stared at the shadows of wooden beams in the ceiling. Sweat covered her face and her head burned with fever.

"E'lisea?" Niscene whispered in the darkness.

But the queen was gone.

TENTH

ALL WAS QUIET save for the Sense, which called to her like always. Niscene's eyes slowly closed and she reached out for it. The Sense flooded into her in that familiar way, like wine filling a cup. Still, her head spun and her stomach threatened to upend itself, but both sensations quickly ebbed as the Sense settled, providing its sweet succor as it pulsed within her. Niscene clung to it as if clinging to life.

How could she? Niscene wondered. How was such a thing even possible? The thought of someone being able to reach through her to wield the power and magik of her Sense made her want to retch – and rage. Such a violation.

If what the queen said was true, then she merely saved Niscene from one rape with another. And one far more intimate and despicable. Niscene's body had been taken and violated many times, but never the Sense that lived on the fringes of her mind. The one place she always believed no one could invade.

"How could you?" she asked aloud in the darkness of her room.

Niscene stared at the shapes behind her eyelids as she listened to the Sense sing to her. The eyelid shadows played their nighttime games while a strange pang rose up and pressed against her chest. *"You were better than in my dreams."* She tried swallowing, but the ache persisted, and spread throughout her body like a poison.

Surely, dawn was near.

Two days. That is how long E'lisea said she had been unconscious. It meant the full moon would rise the following evening. *"She dies at the next full moon."* The command of Ash'an Rah was like a brand in her soul, hissing and burning as she remembered it. *Must she?* Niscene asked of the memory.

It gave no answer.

The hours passed and sleep came and went, engulfing Niscene in fits of restless slumber.

When she did sleep, Niscene was haunted by dreams. In one, she was a little girl again, being raped by her brother's despicable friends while Login himself watched in the corner, his lips turned upward in that half-grin. She cried out and suddenly E'lisea appeared. The glow of the Sense pulsed around the queen in a beautiful show of blue-green light. With one powerful spell, Login and his friends vanished. E'lisea's Sense glow then winked out, and she dropped to the floor to comfort Niscene with a kiss, and to stroke her auburn hair. At the queen's touch, Niscene felt that strange, wonderful sensation rise up in her. Her nostrils picked up the comforting scent of honeysuckle. She swore if the dream ended she would die.

In another dream, Niscene and E'lisea were in their upstairs room in the Midnight Court. Their hair and limbs and bodies were tangled together beneath the white sheets. The moon shone full and dull through the window, its light shrouded in the familiar rufescent haze. Niscene held her Sense, as did the queen. E'lisea's masked face appeared, blue eyes bold and beautiful and full of desire. The queen's lips touched Niscene's and she melted into them.

Her Sense sputtered and shifted; then her mind, body, and aura exploded in a panoply of sensation. No longer was there just her Sense, but the queen's, as well – a separate, though similar, pulse of power, sharp and strong, orderly and beautiful. Niscene felt pleasure – the purest and truest pleasure she could imagine. The twin, yet dissimilar, Senses danced and mingled, pulsed and pounded. They sang songs both chilling and beguiling.

All of Niscene's sensations and faculties were enhanced, and set ablaze; she registered the smallest hints of touch and kiss and breath, every silky stroke of the sheet against her naked back and wet press of lips against her neck and chest. It was like she was on fire – and she wanted more.

Suddenly, the fire inside of her burst forth and consumed everything in the room: the sheets, the bed, the floorboards, the chains hanging from the ceiling – even E'lisea. The fire attacked the queen, charred her skin and burned away her black mask. Her ensuing scream shook the world and Niscene cried out her name. Then, the figure that had been E'lisea burning turned a deep blood red; its limbs and shape contorted and reformed, transubstantiating into an ominous, frightening, hooded figure. A pair of fiery eyes hissed as they burned a deep blood red. Ash'an Rah.

With a scream, Niscene awoke drenched in sweat. Despite a lingering fever, she sat up slowly and placed a hand on the bed frame to steady herself. Without thinking, she reached out and seized the Sense. Out of habit, she sighed. The Sense sang a soft melody that floated across her entire being. It was soothing in its way, haunting and beautiful and chaotic and dark. Still, Niscene's mind remained anxious.

Sleep evaded her the rest of the night.

When dawn broke, Niscene finally slept. When she awoke, she remained, immobilized in her room, staring at the ceiling. She mulled the meaning of her dreams as the stabbing pain in her chest grew larger and stronger. She saw E'lisea's face in her mind's eye and longed to touch her, to kiss her, to be with her.

At other times, she would blink, and see the full moon glowing above her head, burning her eyes and seeming to smother her.

Through all of this, the Sense hummed and called to her with its temptations and sweet melodies, with its promises of power and relief. But the only relief Niscene longed for was with the queen.

When the sun finally set and she ventured once more into the crimson haze of the Midnight Court, Niscene tried not to think of what might happen were E'lisea not to show.

Pausing a moment, she gazed skyward at the moon that had just risen as the sun had set. After two nights spent with the queen and two unconscious in her bed – the moon finally shone, round and full, its yellow light tempered by the red mist clinging to every inch of the Midnight Court. The time had come. Niscene shivered. *"She dies at the next full moon."* The words of Ash'an Rah chilled her. *"Do not fail me."* But, would E'lisea show? Doubt seemed to strengthen the sharp pain in her chest. Niscene attempted to swallow it, to force it down. It did not help.

With each step, the doubt and worry and anxiety intensified, pushing, pressing into Niscene's heart and mind. At times, she thought she felt someone following her, just out of sight behind her. But with each furtive glance, she saw no one.

Then, she turned the familiar corner and there, standing at ease looking beautiful and ravishing even in the dull light of the street lamp, was the queen. Relief flooded through Niscene and she let out her long-held breath.

As she approached, a trio of male pillow friends walked up to the queen and began to gyrate against her. They whispered taunts and teases and pleasure promises. Suddenly enraged, Niscene pushed one of the men away from E'lisea. "She is mine," she growled at the lot of them. In unison they turned hard looks on her. The queen said nothing, her lips pressed tight and her bold, blue eyes stoic behind her leather mask.

"Our tongues will melt her sex," said one of the pillow friends, running a thin, elongated finger down the front of the queen's green gown, which seemed to shimmer even in the Midnight Court's red haze. The queen made no visible reaction. "Our cocks will fill her."

"Fill her," the other two echoed, positioning themselves on either side of E'lisea like sentinels. They each grabbed one of the queen's milky white arms possessively then ran her hands over themselves. E'lisea's face remained unreadable as she allowed the men to toy with her.

Niscene's face hardened. She took another step closer and seized the Sense. "I told you," she said menacingly. "She. Is. *Mine!*"

All of a sudden, a sharp slicing sound hissed, cutting through the vermilion air and, in unison, the three pillow friends cried out in pain. They grabbed between their legs and fell to their knees on the cobbled street. They folded into themselves, whimpering like babes who cried for their mothers.

Niscene barely spared a glance for the mewling men as she stepped over them to stand face to face with the masked queen.

"You truly are wicked," said E'lisea, her voice was sharp, but not harsh. She stared down at the three emasculated men with a mild curiosity.

"More than you know," said Niscene, her heart pumping hard. She thrust her hand in E'lisea's face. The queen stared at it then regarded her, blue eyes betraying nothing from behind the black mask. She tilted her head to the side as if in deep contemplation. Finally, she shook it slowly then laughed aloud as though she had just watched a mummer's farce. It was a genuine laugh – music to Niscene's ears.

"As if I would choose anyone but you," said E'lisea, grasping Niscene's hand and bringing it to her lips. "Besides," she said, lowering the hand. "Men and their cocks bore me."

Glaring down at the men moaning in pain on the cobblestones, the queen traced one of her slippered feet along one of them. She then heaved a strong kick into the man, eliciting a fresh grunt of pain. With a sniff, she led Niscene away down the street.

Holding the queen's hand, Niscene felt a tingle shoot through her body. As they walked the hazy streets, she glanced coyly at E'lisea. A day spent dwelling on the woman's use of the *Sei'na* and how she violated her meant nothing now that they were together again. Nor could the full moon, that ominous orb hanging overhead like a watchful eye, extinguish the feeling. Being in E'lisea's presence stirred something in Niscene she could not place, a strange, wonderful notion that not even the Sense could mimic.

Beyond the ravenous desire that craved once more to be unleashed, there was a tenderness, a fondness or affection. Niscene took a deep breath, inhaling the now familiar scent of honeysuckle, and smiled. Nowhere else did she wish to be.

The queen caught her staring at her, and gave her hand a squeeze.

When they shut and locked the door to their room, Niscene could not hold back any longer. Pushing the other woman onto the round bed, she straddled her, laying an impassioned and desirous kiss upon the masked queen. E'lisea was submissive and eager as any newly married maiden. As Niscene's hands and mouth explored and found familiar places, the queen let out soft moans, but allowed her to do what she wished.

"I am yours," the queen managed between gasps. "Take me! Oh, gods, take me, mistress!"

Niscene's hands slid, down and up, her fingernails gently scratching E'lisea's body, her full red lips kissing, tongue tasting. Her hands brushed against the black leather mask veiling the woman's face. Without a thought, she maneuvered her hands to untie it. The queen made no move to stop her.

With the mask removed, Niscene sat back to behold the queen. Even in the room's dim light, E'lisea's famed beauty was evident. Her high cheek bones and big, blue eyes all framed by her strawberry blonde curls. It made Niscene want her even more.

She lost herself in the sheets with the queen, with this woman she was sent to kill but who had unleashed strange, dormant desires within her. On the margins of her consciousness, she heard a familiar song. A far-off melody that she could reach out and touch if she wished. But she refrained. Instead, she fell toward it, falling deeper, deeper until she embraced it as before.

The Sense flowed into her with its chaotic splendor. She did not have to seize or cling to it; rather, she knew it was an extension of herself, something that always had been, always would be. They embraced, Niscene and the Sense, like lifelong lovers.

"Yes!" she cried, and the Sense reverberated through her. Between the Sense and the queen, pleasure was all Niscene knew, all that mattered.

When climax came, Niscene's vision burst into a

spectacle of color and sensation. Her back arched; she let out a sharp, gasping moan as the queen's pretty face buried deeper between her legs. A harried breath later, she let out a powerful, ecstatic scream.

In the stillness that followed, the two women lay, sweaty and spent, wrapped in each other's arms. Their breaths were heavy and rapid and content. A tingle ran down Niscene's spine as she let go of the Sense. The sudden emptiness spread like a winter chill across her body. She shivered despite herself.

Beside her, E'lisea noticed. "A chill?" the queen asked, bemused. She adjusted slightly and pulled Niscene closer. "There, now, mistress," she said, leaning in for a kiss. "I shall keep you warm."

Niscene nuzzled her head into the queen's shoulder. "Oh, yes," she sighed. Her mind swirled and her heart raced. Oh, this woman. Oh, this queen. How she had entranced her. Never had Niscene known such pleasure was possible. Never, in the innumerable times she'd been made to fuck a man, had she felt the ecstasy and joys she did when with E'lisea. The tenderness, the delectation. If she could but remain with the queen always.

"I would fuck you every night if I could," E'lisea whispered. "If I could, I'd bring you home with me and fuck you forever."

"I doubt your kingly husband would approve of such an arrangement," Niscene said.

The queen bit her lip a moment as if giving the idea deep consideration. "No, he would not," she said with a shake of her head. E'lisea then raised herself up on an elbow and gazed curiously at Niscene. Mirth and mischief flashed in her blue eyes and a coquettish grin spread across her velvet lips. "But only if he found out. Men are such fools, you know. Kings more so." She laughed before lifting up her hands to cup Niscene's face. She laid a gentle kiss on her lips.

When she pulled away, she laughed again. "My kingly husband, the fool." Her grin faded into a sigh. "He always says he loves me, but I've never believed it. He cares more for his crown than he does for me or my desires."

"Then, he truly is a fool," said Niscene.

E'lisea regarded her, blue eyes sharp. "Yes, he is," she said.

The queen gently stroked Niscene's left cheek a

moment. Niscene shivered. E'lisea then traced her fingers downward, adding a subtle circular motion as she reached Niscene's chest. "Of course, I could bring you home with me," said the queen. "He'd never suspect." As her hand journeyed down her body, Niscene's head craned back; her body went taut and trembled. Soon, E'lisea's fingers were just below Niscene's navel. "After all, I am well versed at keeping secrets from my husband."

"Yes," panted Niscene.

The queen leaned forward. As she touched a soft kiss to Niscene's quivering lips, her finger slipped downward and easily into the other woman, conjuring a shudder and moan.

Must I kill you, my sweet queen? wondered Niscene as she arched her back and melted into her.

Unanticipated. All of it. She had traveled to Ramodin as a *Morad'ash,* on a mission to wreak chaos, to strike from the shadows, to steal away with the queen's life beneath the full moon. Outside, she knew, glowing in the sky behind a crimson veil, the moon did shine, round and full. If she were to fulfill her duty, it must be tonight. But how could she now, after these past few days? Somewhere in the darkest corners of her consciousness, something stirred. *Do what must be done.*

"And to think," E'lisea said when she had finished. "Five days ago, you shuddered at my touch."

The two women stood beside the round bed in the middle of the dark room. In her hands, Niscene held the fetters. "I still do," she replied, clasping the manacle around E'lisea's wrists. "And now it's time for you to pay for such things." She took a step back, reaching out to seize the Sense.

"Give me what I deserve, mistress," the queen said, pathetically.

Niscene flicked her wrist and the chains moved, hoisting E'lisea above the bed. Her arms pulled taut over her head, and her toes barely scratched the sheets.

The Sense undulated within her, and Niscene relished its sweet power. But then, just as she prepared her first strike, a hard pounding came at the door. Niscene froze and the queen gasped. Then came a loud muffled voice. Then another. Men's voices. Angry voices. Niscene heard E'lisea's name. The queen heard it, too. She gasped again.

"Gods, no! How?" she asked.

Again, someone pounded on the door – louder this time.

"Open up!" came a man's voice. "In the name of the king – open this door!"

ELEVENTH

"IN THE NAME of King Paeter," the man shouted again. "Open this door!"

E'lisea squirmed overhead. "Please!" she hissed. "I don't know how he found me. I must've...I was care...oh, *gods*!"

Bemused, Niscene regarded the panicky queen, squirming about above her like a fish on a hook. She turned toward the door as another hard pounding rattled it on its hinges.

"Mistress, *please!*" E'lisea screeched. "Paeter will *kill* me! Let me down! We must run away!"

Watching the queen fall into a kind of fearful madness gave Niscene a curious pause. Just moments earlier, this woman had expressed such boldness, such confidence, inviting the pleasure mistress into her own bed at the palace, and eager to be beaten to within an inch of her life. Now, she wriggled about like a worm, desperate to flee. What happened to the woman who used the *Sei'na* against a trio of would-be rapers, making them scream and beg for mercy?

"Open this *bloody* door!" the man outside the room shouted again. What followed was the muffled sound of a struggle, accompanied by the soft scream of steel being pulled from sheaths.

Something finally shook loose inside of Niscene. She would not allow some fool man, king or no king, take her – or the queen for that matter. The Midnight Court was no place for the queen of the realm. Perhaps her sudden fear was legitimate. Perhaps not. What would happen to the queen herself was unclear. But what of the pleasure mistress with whom they found her? It was time to act. Tightening her hold on the Sense, Niscene's mind cleared and sharpened.

"Oh, gods and devils, what's happening out there?" E'lisea moaned, trying to crane her neck and maneuver as best she could while hanging in the air.

Annoyed, Niscene gave her majesty a hard slap of air across her bare back. The woman gasped at the sudden blow. "What are you doing?" But another hard blow struck her.

"Quiet," hissed Niscene. She unleashed another strike across the queen's beautiful face. "We are mistress and subservient. Now, be silent – and relish your pain."

Stupefied, E'lisea went quiet as Niscene hit her again. Then again. Harder this time. The strike opened up a cut above the queen's left eye. *Not enough,* thought Niscene. Gritting her teeth, she let loose another whip of air. Then another. And another. She beat the queen mercilessly, drawing blood and bruising her face. E'lisea did not wince or cry out.

Suddenly, the door burst open. A figure entered. With aid of the moonlight shining through the window, Niscene saw it was a slender man in black attire. He held a short sword in his left hand; something glistened off the blade. Niscene's eyes flashed to a small heap behind the newcomer before focusing on him again. The Sense swirled throughout her; its song chaotic and on edge.

The man regarded Niscene cautiously then his eyes moved around the room, settling on the queen. He gestured with his chin. "Let her down," he said. "Now." He pointed his sword at her menacingly.

Niscene laughed. "Men and their swords," she said. She shook her head. Then, with a flick of her wrist, the sword flew from the man's hand and across the room, where it clattered to the floor.

The intruder stiffened at the sudden loss of his weapon, but did not back down. "In the name of the king, release that woman," he said, stepping further into the room. Closer now, Niscene could make out the man's sharp features, including a nose that jutted straight out from his face.

Above them, E'lisea let out a sharp gasp. With lightning quickness, Niscene let loose a blow across her face. "Quiet, woman!" she hissed.

"It is treason to strike the queen," the man said.

Niscene scoffed. "Queen?" She let out a long, sardonic laugh. "This woman is no queen." She strode confidently over to E'lisea, the Sense undulating through her like ocean waves during a thunderstorm. Eyes fixed on the stranger, she lifted a hand and teasingly ran her fingers up and down the queen's leg. Then, with a dark smile and snap of her fingers, a whip of air struck E'lisea across her bottom. The queen yelped with pleasure as fresh blood blossomed on her body. Niscene folded her arms across her chest. "My *sa'shana* is merely some lady widow come to forget her dead husband, surrendering to long dormant desires, and wishing to lose herself in the pleasures of the Midnight Court."

"Hardly," said the man, unconvinced. "Her lip may be fat and bloody, her eyes red and veiled in shadow." His face hardened as he stepped closer. "But I know mine own sister!"

Overhead, the queen wheezed. *"Dygon?* How did you...?" She trailed off.

"Yes, E'lisea," the man said. "Are you all right?" He glared at Niscene. "Has she hurt you?"

He did not bother to hide his dismissive tone, which only served to enrage Niscene, and the Sense, which still swirled like a storm wind within her. Brother or not, she would make him pay for such insolence.

"No! Mistress, please. Don't!" E'lisea said. "My brother...a *fool*...but he..." Her words came between shallow breaths. "P-please. P...Paeter."

Curse that blood d'ongrata, thought Niscene. Biting her tongue so hard she tasted blood, Niscene stared daggers at the queen's brother. If he were confused by this exchange, he hid it well. *And curse you, brother to the queen!* With a wave of her hand, Niscene undid the fetters clasped around E'lisea's wrists, then reluctantly let go of the Sense. The sweetness of the magik evaporated like water in the sun. The familiar emptiness rose up, threatening to swallow her whole. She shivered despite the sheen of sweat upon her forehead.

Free from the shackles, the queen collapsed like a house of cards. She fell in a heap upon the bed and did not move. Her brother ran to her side but suddenly she lifted a shaky hand to stay him.

"No," she said in a raspy sort of voice. "Please...it's...it's...all right."

The familiar blue-green glow briefly enveloped the queen as she seized the Sense. Then, taking a deep breath, she worked her magik, sewing herself back together with the precision of a skilled seamstress. Cuts and lacerations disappeared as her skin stitched itself; bruises faded as though they never had been.

"By the gods!" the queen's brother exclaimed. "E'lisea?" His eyes widened in surprise then narrowed in skepticism. He stepped back, uncertain. "How? What?" He threw a wary, accusatory finger at Niscene. "You!"

"Leave my mistress be, Dygon," said E'lisea. Her voice no longer sounded raspy and her breathing was no longer labored. She stood and let out a long, languid stretch, as if waking from a restful sleep. "Yes, much better," she said, more to herself than the others. The fear that had only moments ago nearly driven her to hysterics was gone, replaced by that familiar mischief and playfulness Niscene knew so well. She stretched again, pulling her arms behind her back, a motion that thrust out her chest. Her brother, who quickly realized his sister was nude, averted his eyes.

"Oh, Dygon, as if we did not bathe together as children," E'lisea said with a cluck of her tongue. She looked at Niscene. "I told you he was a fool." With a laugh, the queen bent down near the bed to find her clothing.

The man named Dygon ignored his sister's insult. Despite the urgency with which he burst into the room, the man suddenly appeared calm and at ease, waiting for E'lisea to dress. His eyes moved about the room, regarding anything and everything save his sister. He observed everything – from the wooden floorboards to the texture of the bed sheets, the soft creaking of the shackles swaying above his head to Niscene herself, who stood, hands balled into fists at her side, watching him, her mind racing with questions and concerns over this strange man who tracked the queen here. And on the night of the full moon.

Nude though she was, the man leveled his eyes on Niscene and did not look away. Rather, he scrutinized her – not as a man tantalized by her nakedness, but with the shrewd detachment of a trader or merchant evaluating a piece of merchandise. His beady, deep-set eyes, unreadable, traced upward from her feet until they met Niscene's own steely gaze. The Sense stirred and called to her, its usual haunting appeal having developed a more frenetic edge. This man could be trouble, Niscene knew. Neither one looked away until the queen spoke.

"Your assistance, please, mistress," said E'lisea, stepping between her brother and Niscene. Her strawberry blonde curls were damp and her skin again was milk white and unblemished. She offered her back to Niscene, who, without objection, lifted her hands. Methodically, she hooked each of the tiny hooks on the queen's dress.

When Niscene finished, the queen tossed her hair over her shoulders and lifted herself to her full height. She glared at the man, Dygon. "So, brother," said E'lisea, a noticeable edge to her voice. "How did you find me?" She stabbed a finger square in the man's chest.

Dygon glanced curiously at his sister's accusatory finger, pressed hard against his chest, just below his heart. He said nothing. Not at first, anyway. In the dim light, his face, sharp and angular, was hazy; his expression remained unreadable, detached. His countenance gave away nothing of what went on behind his eyes. *What are you thinking, fool man?* Niscene silently wondered as she watched over the queen's shoulder. She braced herself. The queen may have been unbothered by her brother's presence and strange detachment, but something tickled at the back of Niscene's mind, putting her on edge. Part of the Oath whispered in her mind: *The world shall no not my name nor my face.* As if somehow reading her mind, the man, Dygon, met her eyes. On the fringes of her mind, The Sense called to her with its dark melody.

After a moment, the queen's brother looked away and addressed his sister. "You know what your husband pays me to do," he said flatly.

Without warning, the queen lifted a hand and slapped her brother across the face. The hard *crack* made Niscene jump. Dygon remained where he was, unmoved and seemingly unperturbed.

"That is not an answer," E'lisea said, visibly agitated. At her sides, her hands twitched. Then, she slapped him again. Other than a slight flaring of his nostrils, the man again made no reaction, nor any motion to defend himself. The queen hit him again. "How did you find me?"

For the briefest of moments, Dygon's eyes flashed toward Niscene. He pressed his lips together into a thin line, almost hesitant. "Answer the question, brother," demanded the queen.

Dygon again looked at his sister. "I followed you," he said.

E'lisea threw back her head and laughed harshly. "Clearly," she said, gesturing with her hands. "You are here, are you not?" She stepped right into the man's face, standing on her toes to get close. The edge in her voice sharpened. "*How* did you *find* me?"

Dygon folded his arms across his chest and sighed. "You think you're clever sneaking out the servants entrance?"

"You bloody bastard!" E'lisea cried, hitting him in the shoulder. "You bribed one of them to tell, didn't you?"

The man said nothing.

"Seven bloody hells!" she exclaimed. E'lisea again slapped her brother across the face. Other than a brief blink of the eyes, he still made no reaction or motion to stop her. "Is there no one in the palace you don't...?" But she stopped dead before finishing. "Oh, gods!" Her blue eyes widened and she covered her mouth with her hands. "You must not tell the king!" she said, barely above a whisper.

Terror was thick in her voice. E'lisea turned away and began to pace nervously a moment, then turned back to her brother. "Please, Dygon. Paeter must not know about any of this." She gestured about the dark, dank room. "If he did..." She turned her head away for a moment, thinking, then looked again at her brother. "You cannot tell him," she commanded. "I forbid it! You hear me?"

Her brother said nothing. Indeed, the man's countenance was as emotionless as a corpse. The man's ability to shroud his emotions so well made Niscene anxious. She did not trust him. When his eyes gazed over his sister's shoulder and into hers, Niscene nearly seized the Sense to strike him dead.

"What would Paeter do if he were to learn of your..." Dygon again focused his eyes on his sister. "...dalliances?"

"He would kill me," the queen whimpered.

A short sniffing sound, almost like a laugh, escaped the man's lips. It was the most emotion he had shown since barging into the room. "Your kingly husband loves you, dear sister," he said. "You are the mother to his children and his queen. He adores you."

It was E'lisea's turn to snort. "Love me, adore me. You truly believe if Paeter discovered that I came to the Midnight Court, those things would stay his hand?"

Niscene watched the man's jaw clench ever so slightly, though his overall countenance remained unchanged. The two siblings stared at each other, daring the other to look away first. Niscene could not see E'lisea's expression, but she noticed, over the queen's shoulder, a mild twitch of Dygon's lips. Then he waved away the queen's query.

"While I truly doubt your conviction that the king would...*harm* you, sister, your marriage bed – and anything you may happen to do away from it – are none of my concern." His eyes flashed toward Niscene.

"Then you won't speak of this with Paeter?" asked E'lisea.

His eyes lingered a moment longer on Niscene before looking back at the queen. "No," he said.

The queen's body shuddered with relief. "Maker's mercy, Dygon," she said with a sigh. "Thank you." She kissed her brother on the cheek.

The man nodded then raised an eyebrow. "But you did not answer my question."

E'lisea's eyes narrowed. "What question?" She again was on edge.

Dygon's calm voice developed an edge of its own. "Do not play coy with me, sister," he said. He circled her, waving a hand up and down. "A moment ago, you were bloody and bruised. Now? How did you...*heal* yourself?"

The queen hesitated then exchanged a look with Niscene.

"Was it her?" Dygon asked, following his sister's gaze. He did not bother to hide the scowl that suddenly appeared on his face when he again looked Niscene up and down.

"No," E'lisea said, drawing her brother's focus back to her. "The truth is..." She closed her eyes for a brief moment, hesitating. "I can hear the Sense."

"The *Sense*?" The shock in the man's voice was clear. His eyes widened then narrowed. "E'lisea – you can...wield *magik*?" He stared at her as if seeing her for the first time.

Slowly, the queen's head bobbed up and down. "Yes," she said, reaching for her brother's hands. He tensed as if burned, but relaxed, allowing her to take them. "I heard it for the first time as a little girl," she said. E'lisea threw a sidelong glance at Niscene, who remembered well her first time hearing the sweet, tempestuous melody at the margins of her consciousness. Like a sprite or spirit you knew was there but could never look upon directly, the Sense had called to her in the midst of her darkest moments. And called to her still.

"Maker's mercy, sister!" Dygon exclaimed. "All this time?"

She nodded. "I learned to control and use it properly – though it was difficult. The stories are not exaggeration. I even became quite adept at healing," the queen said. Nodding toward the rusty, creaky chains hanging above the bed, she added, "It has...had its uses."

"Did our parents know?" her brother asked.

E'lisea's face pinched up as if insulted, and she laughed derisively. "Are you mad? Of course not," she said. "No one in the family did." She sighed. "Until now."

Brother and sister fell silent, and Niscene stood as observer to this most peculiar of family dramas. Through the window, a beam of dull, reddish moonlight glowed, reminding her that time was running out. Through the walls, there came a loud, repetitive pounding, along with a woman's loud moans and cries.

"Does the king know?" asked Dygon.

Immediately, E'lisea dropped the man's hands as if burned, and scowled at him. "You are mad, aren't you?" she said, stepping away from her brother. "What do you think?" She turned her back to him, wrapping her arms around herself. "You know Paeter's views on magik."

Dygon opened his mouth to respond but stopped himself. He looked at Niscene. "Is it wise to speak of such things in front of this one?" He examined her in the shadows, judging her, dehumanizing her. The Sense howled and she nearly seized it. "The Midnight Court is—"

A harsh slap split the air, cutting off the man. This time, he raised a hand to his cheek and winced.

"Say not a word about her," E'lisea said. Her bold, blue eyes burned as she stared daggers at her brother. "Paeter makes no secret of his disdain for the magiks," she continued. "He avoids wizards and witches of his own accord, even banning sorcerers and tricksters from performing at court. He only tolerates Philosophers because he must. You know this." The queen jabbed a finger into Dygon's chest, then threw her hands into the air. "Everyone knows this. Even she." E'lisea thrust a finger in Niscene's direction.

"I am aware of the king's thoughts on magik, yes," Dygon said, again glancing at Niscene out of the corner of his eye.

The queen then stooped down and picked up her black mask. She placed it across her face and tied it behind her head. Cocking her head to the side, she glared at her brother, her eyes peering out from behind the mask. "And what of yours?" E'lisea asked.

The queen's brother hesitated, though he tried to hide it. "All these years," he said. He began to pace around the room. "My own sister. Magik…"

"The Sense does not change who I am, Dygon," E'lisea said.

"Doesn't it?" he replied, stopping near the window. "You no doubt know how to work the elements and perform tricks and spells – and gods know what else." He looked down then knelt to pick up something. Niscene bit her tongue when she saw the man rise with his short sword in his hand. Using the curtains by the window he wiped clean the blade then slid it silently into its sheath at his side.

"Yes, but I am still *me*," the queen insisted.

Dygon said nothing. Instead, he turned to glance out the window. Then something drew his eyes to the wall. He reached out and took the whip from its hook.

"And what of this?" he asked, brandishing the whip.

"Is this what you prefer? To be beaten like some whore in the Midnight Court? You're the queen, E'lisea!" He examined the whip briefly before throwing it hard to the floor. It connected with a loud *thump*. The queen's brother spread his arms wide and moved his head about the room. "Who could find pleasure in any of this?" he asked.

In an instant, E'lisea stood before her brother, chin thrust into the air as she glared at him. At her sides, Niscene saw, the queen's hands intermittently clench and unclench into fists. "Me," said E'lisea. "I find immense pleasure in all of this." She raised a hand and slapped her brother hard across his face. The crack of hand on cheek made even Niscene wince. In the dull light of the moon, she saw the man's cheek turn a varying shade of red. But he made no move to soothe or touch it. He merely gazed down at his sister over his long, protruding nose.

"Who are you to judge the pleasures I seek?" the queen demanded. She slapped him once more, on the other cheek this time, so his face took on a ruddy complexion. "Who are you to judge anything about me?"

The man called Dygon, brother to the queen, still said nothing. He merely stood, staring at E'lisea, no discernible expression on his sharp-featured face. This non-reaction further infuriated the queen and she let loose another slap. Then another. And another. Her anger quickly boiled over and Niscene watched in morbid wonderment as the other woman embraced her Sense and began whipping her brother with air and magik and her own fists. Once, twice, thrice across his face. Again and again, each blow exploding, ripping, breaking the skin, imbued with more intensity and power than the last. Still, her brother brooked no reaction on his face, now bloodied and bruised and swollen.

The queen continued her assault.

Niscene watched the display with amazement. During their short time together, she had seen the queen submissive and playful, wild and wicked. Even fearful. But the ferocity and sheer viciousness with which she attacked her own brother revealed yet another side of her. No dainty, spoiled monarch was she. No. She was something far more menacing. Something far more alluring. Something far more dangerous.

With one final blow, the queen gave up her Sense and stumbled backward. Her shoulders slumped and her head lolled forward above her chest. She sighed heavily, inhaling and exhaling for several seconds until she lifted a hand to wipe at her eyes. With a glance over her shoulder, she collapsed onto the bed; its tired mattress groaned softly.

Niscene watched as the queen's brother raised a hand to his face. He grimaced at the slightest touch. He looked a bloody, beaten mess – as if he had lost a tavern brawl. A thousand tiny cuts adorned his face while streaks of blood spidered in various directions. His left eye was dark with bruising, his lower lip was split and swollen.

"E'lisea…" he said.

"Stop," the queen said, standing. With a fierce look in her eyes, she approached her brother. Again, Niscene saw the woman embrace the Sense, the soft blue-green glow enveloping her for the briefest moment. Then, using one hand to hold the man's head still, E'lisea ran her other hand over his blemished face, tracing with the softest of touches the scratches, lacerations, and bruises. With each stroke and touch, Dygon's injuries melted away as if no such wounds ever existed. When she finished, E'lisea let go of her Sense and tilted her head to examine her work. After several seconds, she let her hand drop to her side.

Hesitantly, Dygon lifted a hand to his face. Gently at first, but soon he moved his jaw and ran his hand all over his countenance, brushing off some flecks of dried blood.

"What did...?"

"I healed you," E'lisea said. "People would ask too many questions if you returned with a bruised and bloody face. Here." She strode past the man to reach for the wash basin. She dampened a small hand towel in the water and handed it to her brother. "Wash off the blood," she said. "Then leave."

In silence, the queen's brother brought the towel to his face and washed it clean. Satisfied, the queen took the towel and tossed it behind him where it fell with a soft *plunk* into the wash basin.

"You will speak no word of this," said E'lisea. "To anyone." The queen then pointed a finger at the door. "Now go."

Niscene watched as the pointy-nosed man regarded his sister, the queen. The shock of learning his sister's secret was gone, replaced by his original blank, detached expression. What went on behind his eyes was a mystery.

Then there was the queen, bothering not at all to hide

her emotions. A hard look in her eye, she glared at her brother. Neither spoke.

For her part, Niscene stuck to the shadows of the room, silent as an assassin waiting to strike. Even with one side masking emotion, the tension between brother and sister was palpable. Niscene's mind recalled the spotty memories of the other night. The would-be rapers screaming into the night. *It was all her.* Did the fool brother not comprehend that his sister could kill him with a thought? And she wouldn't even need to use the *Sei'na.* He was as helpless as a newborn babe. The Sense swirled at the edge of her mind, calling to her, singing its sweet chaotic melody.

"It is time you leave," E'lisea said. The edge in her voice cut through the tension like an assassin's blade. "Do not follow me again. Leave us. *Now.*"

The man nodded, but said nothing. He looked away from his sister and stepped toward the door. He spared a curious glance for Niscene as he passed. She scowled at him. Without a parting word, the queen's brother strode through the doorway, closing the door behind him.

Twelfth

When her brother had gone, E'lisea approached Niscene and cupped her cheek. A thin, sad smile spread across her lips then vanished into a sigh. "My brother…" The queen trailed off. She dropped her hand and stared over her shoulder at the door. "He…" But she again failed to finish her thought. After several moments, she inclined her head and smiled another thin smile. "You truly are remarkable, mistress," she said. Then she leaned in and laid a soft kiss on Niscene's cheek.

Niscene closed her eyes, relishing the queen's soft lips against her skin. She took a deep breath, inhaling the woman's familiar, intoxicating scent. Remarkable? Never had anyone ever paid her such a compliment. Men had spoken many empty words when she was whored out by her brother – the false tenderness all men resorted to in the moments immediately after they received what they wanted. But the queen – her sweet words were neither false nor empty. Rather, they sounded true. When E'lisea spoke such words, Niscene felt a stirring in her heart not even the Sense could mimic. She wished nothing more than to lose herself in the queen. Again and again. Over and over. *Am I truly to steal your life, my queen? As you have stolen my heart?*

Finally – sadly – E'lisea pulled away, ending the kiss far too soon. Niscene sighed deeply as the warmth of the queen ebbed, replaced by a sudden chill that pricked her skin, giving rise to goose flesh. Her eyes fluttered open with a shudder.

E'lisea had wandered over to the window, where she gazed out at the crimson-colored sky. The light of the moon, full and ominous, shone through, casting the queen's beautiful face in a melancholy glow.

Niscene stared longingly at the other woman, a powerful ache building inside of her. *Is this the end?* she wondered. *Is this the moment I've been waiting for?* The moment she now wished had never come?

The moon was full and her command was clear: *"She dies at the next full moon."* She trembled as a bead of sweat tickled the back of her neck. Niscene brushed a hand across her brow, suddenly warm. A sense of dread rose up then, threatening to consume her. Niscene squeezed shut her eyes to steel herself – but a sudden flash of fear forced them open. *What was that?* She thought something – or someone – had been there, just over her shoulder. She blinked. There it was again. Had the queen's brother returned without their knowing? Daring not to breathe, Niscene slowly turned her head to glimpse behind her. Only empty shadows. Strangely, the Sense was quiet.

"Perhaps it is best we end our session early," said E'lisea, whose voice penetrated the dread and foreboding threatening to overtake Niscene.

She swallowed. "As you say." Without another word, she dressed, and the women left the room for the last time.

As they ventured out into the night, Niscene's hand slipped into E'lisea's with ease. It sent a pleasing shock through her body and helped her temporarily forget the weight of the full moon overhead. The spring air was cool and the red haze of the Midnight Court hung low over the brick and stone pleasure houses. The aroma of sex and sweat filled the air. And something else. Shadows and figures danced and pranced down alleyways, and silhouetted in dimly lit windows. After several nights in the Midnight Court, Niscene tried to pay them no mind. Yet, she could not. Every movement, every shadow and sound that floated across the vermilion air caused Niscene to wince and throw furtive looks in every direction. That pang of sadness pressed deeper into her chest, but so, too, did that notion of foreboding again rise up, threatening to envelop her, drown her forever. Niscene blinked and a fresh flash of fear shook her. *What was that?* With a jerk of her head, she glanced behind her.

Over her shoulder lay nothing but the cool, crimson-covered streets.

With each step they took, every move closer to the street corner where they would part ways, Niscene's insides twisted into knots. Her throat tightened. *I do not want to leave her*, she realized. *I cannot leave her!* How had it happened? She thought she heard the Sense sing to her, but it sounded…

off-key, jarring somehow. She ignored it, instead attempting to focus on the queen's hand, which she held firmly. She managed to look at her, at the color of her hair, and the angle of her face. E'lisea caught her eyes.

Then, from somewhere far off, yet intimately near, a voice spoke: *Kill her...*

It came like a whisper on the wind, soft and low. It came not from the Sense, for she knew that voice well. This...was something else. Someone else. But what – or who?

With her free hand Niscene wiped at her brow, suddenly wet with sweat. Dizzy, she stopped, hoping to steel herself. Was she falling ill? Sweat trickled into her eyes and she squeezed them shut – then gasped. Somewhere in the deepest recesses of her being, she again felt that sense of dread, of foreboding. Quickly, it rose, soon looming over her. Behind her eyelids, a face took shape. A familiar visage. Crying out, she opened her eyes to the world and glanced over her shoulder.

"Mistress, what's wrong?" asked the queen.

Shaking, Niscene peered into the red, hazy darkness behind them, but saw nothing more than the familiar shadows and shapes that made up the Midnight Court. She looked skyward, searching for and finding the moon. She quickly averted her eyes, turning them on the queen. Through the slits of her black mask, E'lisea's blue eyes met hers. Her brow furrowed and she frowned. Driven by a strange fear, Niscene leaned in and kissed her, melting into the other woman. Yes. It felt right. Oh, that she could embrace the queen and never let go.

KILL HER!

The words erupted like a volcano in Niscene's mind. The force caused her to stumble backward down the street. Extending a hand, she steadied herself on a nearby brick wall. Her mind continued to spin and boil, and she fell to her knees.

Fear chased her to the Sense, which called to her over the fiery dread that attacked her mind. Niscene lunged for it, seizing its sweet, haunting power. Pulsing in her, the Sense sang its chaotic melody. That song, like a storm, full of rage and power and magik – Niscene knew it well. That song that had been her constant companion all her life. The unending melody of dark comfort. She clung to the Sense desperately, fearful of the presence that lingered just behind her, lurking like a demon at the limits of her mind.

E'lisea was at her side immediately. "Mistress," she said, alarmed. "What is the matter?"

But Niscene did not answer. Indeed, she could not. Fear, unlike anything she had ever experienced, struck her to the very core of her being. On the street, she knelt, frozen in that place, hands over her eyes in a vain attempt to block it out. But it did no good. Eyes open, eyes closed – she saw him: a shadowy, hooded figure, with two fiery eyes and a brutal, vicious voice, like ice and fire. Ash'an Rah.

"Your life is forfeit in service to Death!" The voice sounded all around her; it enveloped her, shutting out the rest of the world. *"You are Morad'ash! Your life is forfeit! Do what must be done."*

In the darkness, I bind my service. To Death, I pledge my fealty. The words of the Oath echoed in her mind. *All I am and all I was is forfeit to Ash'a.*

A soft late-night breeze blew through the street. Goose pimples pricked Niscene's skin as the wind whistled past her. Disembodied laughs and moans rippled through the air above her head. Her breathing was heavy and quick, and her heart pounded in her chest. Sweat beaded down her forehead and she shivered. She vaguely comprehended that she still clung to the Sense.

From this day, the world will know not my name, nor my face.

"Mistress?" Slowly, Niscene's head turned to regard E'lisea. Worry washed over the queen's beautiful, masked face. "Are you not well?" Her blue eyes were wide and her velvet lips pursed into an expression of concern. She put a hand to Niscene's forehead. "Gods, you're burning up!" E'lisea's hand was cool, a respite from the fever spell in her mind.

Niscene stared at the woman whom she had come to murder for reasons unknown. *I am Morad'ash.* Niscene's head tilted to the side and she grabbed the queen's delicate chin between her fingers. Her eyes focused on the woman's thin, soft lips. Those lips that tasted of honeysuckle.

A flash of guilt struck her then, and she retracted her hand as though bitten. *Run!* Niscene wanted to scream at her. *Get away from me! I've been sent to kill you!* But the words evaporated in a stream of consciousness before they reached her tongue. Her head burned.

From the shadows, shall I strike.

She blinked and Ash'an Rah was there in the median,

his flaming eyes erupting in the recesses of his hood. *"Your life is forfeit,"* his chaotic voice boiled. *"Do what must be done. The Oath binds you."*

No. She wanted to scream it at him. *No!* She did not know what consequence awaited a Morad'ash who failed, but why must E'lisea die? *I love her!* she wanted to shout. The vision just repeated its refrain: *"Do what must be done."*

Conflicting desires swirled and broiled inside of Niscene. To kill the queen, to save the queen – both did battle in her mind like two warriors locked in combat. Which would win? She could not say.

E'lisea tenderly stroked Niscene's forehead, wiping away sweat. "Mistress, your fever…" The queen trailed off as Niscene reached out to stroke her cheek.

"Please," she choked. "Do not leave me."

"Never," whispered E'lisea. All of a sudden, that familiar blue-green glow enveloped her, then quickly winked out. The queen pressed a cool hand to Niscene's forehead and her skin tingled with magik.

After a moment, the queen took her hand away, frustrated. "Dammit!" she swore. "I can't seem to…you need a healer. And rest. And – I…" E'lisea trailed off a moment, as if in thought. She muttered something about some woman, but the fever spell was on Niscene and she could not make out the queen's exact words.

"I'm bringing you to the palace!" E'lisea said suddenly.

Despite her burning mind, Niscene's eyes widened. "The palace?" she wheezed.

"Yes, the palace," E'lisea said, brushing strands of Niscene's hair out of her eyes. "It is not far. I...I cannot leave you like this. I know someone who can help. I..." She again touched a hand to Niscene's forehead. "I am not leaving you tonight."

So kind, thought Niscene, her mind swirling. *E'lisea. My queen.* She smiled thinly at the other woman. She blinked and again came face to face with Ash'an Rah. But, with a hiss, the vision suddenly melted. Niscene felt a refreshingly cool sensation spread throughout her mind and body. A pleasant shiver ran through her.

"I will keep you cool as best I can until we make it to the palace," E'lisea whispered, placing two fingers on Niscene's forehead. The queen then traced a path down her face. Where her fingers touched, Niscene's face cooled, as if ice had been placed there. The shock of the cooling spell caused her to lose her grip on the Sense, and it slipped away. She barely registered its sudden absence as E'lisea kissed her suddenly cool lips.

Thirteenth

Silence ruled the cavernous hallways of the palace. Dygon, the king's steward and brother to the queen, ascended one of its many sweeping staircases. While his heart beat much faster than normal, and innumerable questions raced through his mind like a winter's wind, he maintained a well-practiced expression of calm detachment. Despite the chaos unfolding inside, his face remained placid, one arm casually gripping the ornate banister while the other hung lazily at his side. Were he to confront someone in the hallways, nothing would appear amiss. All anyone would see was the king's steward, making his way about the palace. In no particular hurry or rush.

Of course, considering the hour, it was doubtful he would run into anyone, particularly in this wing. Still, he maintained his mask of serenity and walked without haste.

The palace was expansive and labyrinthine, its myriad corridors, hallways, stairwells all flexuous and confusing to foreigners and visitors. At times, even confusing to those who called the place home. Dygon, of course, knew every hall and passage. And knew them well.

At the next floor, he turned right and ambled down the hallway, his footsteps echoing softly off the stone walls. Lanterns provided light enough to see by as he strolled. Lanterns imbued by magik. A scowl threatened to shatter Dygon's perfectly blank expression. But he smothered it with a blink.

Magik. An itch tickled Dygon's left cheekbone. *All this time?* The itch intensified, almost to a burn. Around the next corner he stopped in front of a nondescript door. In fact, unless someone did not already know it was there, they would miss it completely. From an inside coat pocket he produced a key and inserted it into the lock. A second later, he slipped into his chambers, locking the door behind him.

He lifted a hand to his cheek and scratched the burning itch.

Once sated, he strode over to an old oil lamp and lit it. Grabbing it by the handle, he stepped in front of a full-body mirror in the corner of the room. Dygon stared at his reflection. His nose protruded from his face like an accusation, something he had learned to use to his advantage. And his eyes, though beady, saw far more than most. He pressed his face close to the mirror and lifted the lamp to illuminate it.

In an uncharacteristic move, he began to flex his facial muscles, making a number of strange expressions to stretch and pull at his skin; his eyes keen and focused, searched and examined. He brought up his free hand to grope and caress his face, pushing and peeling aside the few folds his thin countenance possessed, as though he were a healer looking for a minuscule cut or bruise or something else amiss.

Yet, he found nothing. No scratch. No mark. No bruise or scar, though there ought to be something. His sister had drawn blood, after all. But he was completely healed. An unfamiliar mixture of fear and frustration filled him.

Magik. He mouthed the word. Pulling back from the mirror, he shook his head. *All this time. My own sister.* Suddenly, a wave of exhaustion washed over him. Turning from the mirror, Dygon set down the lamp on a small table then sat in a nearby chair. He leaned back and his head slowly lolled against a cushion. Shadows played tricks in the low ceiling, assisted by the faint lamp light. Dawn still was a good many hours away and he had not slept. But it likely would be a while until he did.

Dygon first noticed E'lisea sneak away into the city five nights before, the same night Paeter left on his journey north. Driven by his lifelong desire to know everything, Dygon followed her at once, but quickly lost her past the market in the King's Square. Immediately, he set someone to watch her quarters and run to him with news of her return. He quickly learned she snuck away every night, just before sunset, using the servants' passages to avoid detection. *A clever move, sister.* If anyone were to question her absence, who would search the servants' domain for the queen?

Further still, who would have known E'lisea sought

the Midnight Court? That den of debauchery, whose history stretched farther back than the Unified Kingdom itself, where noble and ignoble alike converged in every act of wantonness and desire one could imagine. Dygon's eye twitched.

The Midnight Court. Where E'lisea went to seek the pleasures of pain. E'lisea, his sweet, little sister. Dygon would have laughed had he not seen it with his own eyes: hanging in the middle of the room, arms stretched above her head, clasped in iron fetters, blood striped across her naked body. Dygon pushed the memory from his mind as he lifted himself from the chair. He stepped to the door and dumped his hands into the wash basin that sat on a stand next to it. The water was lukewarm. He lifted his hands and ran them over his face. Despite its temperature and stale taste, the water was refreshing in its way.

While Dygon loved, obeyed, and was in service to the king, Paeter would hear not a whisper of his queen's activities – at least not from the steward himself. The king tolerated the existence of the Midnight Court in his city. But just barely. Men desiring the warm comforts of a woman, he understood. But the Midnight Court was far more than a mere whorehouse district. Dygon blinked.

Such secrets and more had he kept for his sister. As she did for him in return. *Nothing is stronger than sibling blood.* Those were the words their father had said to Dygon when he first viewed his baby sister so many years ago. Before their father sent his son away.

With a heavy sigh, Dygon shook away the hurtful remembrance, bringing his focus back to the present. He began to pace around his room, a habit of his when trying to make sense of something. And much troubled him tonight. Least of which was the queen's apparent propensity for seeking the pleasure of pain. The Midnight Court. Dygon nearly laughed. Were the other pressing matter not of much more import, his mind surely would be turning over the many meanings of his sister's late-night rendezvous.

But E'lisea heard the Sense. She could wield magik. With a thought, she could heal herself of wounds. With a stare, she struck him with whips of air. What else could she do?

Magik, like a rose, could be admired for its beauty, yet also pierce you if handled improperly. *Magik.* His sister.

Such secrets had they shared over the years. But this one. Dygon paused in his pacing to ponder it. She had kept it from him. In all the years, through all the days and nights they spent together, she had kept such a secret. Through their father's illness, and mother's sorrow. Through her wedding and the war. Never once had she let pass her lips word that she heard the Sense.

Magik. Sweet, fierce, beguiling E'lisea. Who always saw more than she let on; behind whose eyes held such cleverness and charm. Always insisting on playing mysterious or bored, even with her brother. Looking back, perhaps Dygon ought not be surprised at learning of such a secret. He scowled – a rare moment of emotion for him, even alone. But, with no one else present, he risked it. Then, he laughed.

"You clever, clever woman," Dygon said, barely audible even to himself. More than 20 years of habit kept him from ever speaking louder than necessary. Trading in secrets and whispers did that to a man. He chuckled softly again. "Magik, and Paeter has never suspected," he said aloud.

Then again, why would the king ever have reason to?

His notions and prejudices against magik were as widely known as his disdain for the Midnight Court. If he could rid the world of spells and wizards and sorcerers – especially the Philosophers – he would do so. But even kings are not all-powerful. How would the king react were he to learn of his wife's power? Would it change how he felt about his queen? Dygon knew how fiercely Paeter loved E'lisea. What would he say? What would he do?

As the questions raced across his mind, Dygon heard a heavy pounding at the door. He froze immediately, not even daring to breathe.

A moment later, the pounding sounded again. "Oh, seven hells, Dygon!" came a booming and exasperated voice. "Open the bloody door. I know you're awake."

Frowning, but no less guarded, Dygon did as the voice commanded. After all, one did not disobey the king, even when his majesty was unexpected.

Standing on the other side of the door, King Paeter wore a grim expression. He had a raggedy look about him; his dark green eyes were tired. He smelled of the forest, sweat, and death.

"Your majesty," Dygon said, bowing the king into the

room. "You've returned…early." Returned after only five days? Something must have happened.

Despite his appearance, the king strode through the door as if he were the most important man in the world. He very well may have been. With a kingly flare, he flipped his wind-worn red hair over his shoulders and undid the riding cloak tied around his neck.

"Maker's mercy, it's hotter than the endless bloody desert in this room," the king declared, tossing the cloak across a nearby chair. He shook his neck, then gave it a stretch from side to side before collapsing into a seat with blue cushions. He let out a deep, troubled sigh.

"I've water, if you like," Dygon said, refraining from asking the questions that stood at the ready on the tip of his tongue. He shut the door and walked to a water pitcher that sat next to the oil lamp.

The king snorted. "You've no wine with which to greet your king?"

Dygon arched an eyebrow at his friend. "Wine with which to greet your king?" he repeated in a mocking tone. "Do you hear yourself?"

The men shared a laugh before quickly falling silent.

Pressing his lips together, Dygon brought a cup of water to the king, who took it without a word. The steward then sat in a seat opposite his friend and steepled his fingers. Paeter took two long draughts then sighed wearily. His eyes found the oil lamp and gazed into its flame as if it could provide answers to questions only kings were privy to.

Curiosity soon got the better of Dygon and he leaned in to ask, "Why are you returned so early?"

The king scoffed. "Early?" Paeter said. "It's bloody late; nearly dawn, no doubt." He forced a grin, and sipped his water. The grin swiftly vanished. "But if you must know – and, gods be good, if anyone must, it's you – a group of those bloody river clansmen took us by surprise." Paeter stared into his drink, a haunted gleam in his eyes. "Bloody savages," he mumbled before emptying his cup.

Dygon leaned back in his seat. The river clans had intensified their raids in recent months. He gathered their recent boldness might drive them across to the southern side of the river, only a two-day ride north of Ramodin. A problem for another time.

The steward leaned forward. "So you never made it to…?"

"Of course not!" Paeter said, nearly shouting. "Maker's bloody mercy, Dygon! Have you no decency?" He shot a hard look at the other man. "Ten good men died at the hands of those river savages." Paeter shook his head and stared into his empty cup. He sighed.

Dygon blinked and stymied a grimace. *Yes, decency.* He again leaned back in his chair and folded his hands in his lap. He sucked in a deep breath and let it out slowly. "My apologies," he said. "You're right, your majesty. It was..." But whatever it was went unspoken.

"Sometimes," the king said, setting aside his empty cup and fixing a curious look on the steward, "you're too bloody serious for your own good."

You taught me that, old friend. Dygon would never speak such words aloud, of course; but the lessons of war and power and secrets had encased his heart in stone. *The things I have done to ensure stability and peace.* Dygon met his king's eyes. Such orders came at a cost. *You ought to know, my friend.* Dygon knew he did.

"I want you to arrange burial for those slain," Paeter said, drawing Dygon out of his thoughts. "Ensure their widows and sons are well compensated."

"Yes, your majesty," Dygon said respectfully.

The king snorted. "Drop that formality," he said, scrubbing a hand through his red locks. "Are we at court?" He gestured around the room. "I see only a steward's study, in which two old friends sit and talk and drink to their fallen comrades." Paeter tapped the leg of his chair with a boot. "Not that unbearably uncomfortable blue throne nor the room in which it sits." He furrowed his brow and stroked his strong chin. "Are you well, Dygon?"

Well? The river clans become evermore emboldened, your queen seeks pleasure away from your bed, and my sister hears the Sense. Wrinkling his pointy nose, Dygon scratched it then brushed away the king's question. "Just tired," he said. "Who was slain?"

Paeter cleared his throat, then told him. Dygon nodded. "How did the clans get the upper hand?" It made no sense in his mind, which bothered him, like a piece of hard to reach food caught in one's tooth.

"Bloody magik." The king's voice was cold.

Dygon stiffened. *He would kill me.* E'lisea's words echoed in the steward's mind. He brushed a hand over his temple and cheek. Despite himself, he winced. He opened his mouth to speak but caught himself. He cleared his throat, then stood.

"I will call the Philosophers on the morrow," the steward said. The king's return after only a few days away was troubling enough, but where had a savage river tribe learned to wield magik? *Even savages have secrets, it seems.* Dygon swallowed back his annoyance.

"Well," the king said, ignorant of all that went on in Dygon's mind. "No doubt E'lisea has missed me these past few days." Paeter ran a meaty hand through his red hair, then rose from his seat. "Methinks I shall go surprise her."

At mention of the queen, Dygon's mind cleared. He threw a sidelong glance toward his balcony window. Darkness reigned. *How long until dawn?* The king's sudden arrival had caused him to lose track of time.

"It is late. No doubt, the queen is asleep," the steward said, grabbing and refilling the king's empty water cup. "She spent much of the evening entertaining some visiting ladies from the Western Plains. Much wine was drunk, if reports from the kitchens are to be believed." He stepped in front of the king and offered the sweating cup of water, along with a forced wry grin. The story was true enough; the queen had entertained three ladies visiting from the plains. Of course, they merely supped and strolled through the palace gardens until dusk when E'lisea excused herself.

The king brushed aside the proffered drink and chuckled. "Oh, my friend," he said, slapping Dygon's shoulder, which caused some water to spill onto the carpet, "there is much you do not know about your sister."

Maintaining a tempered outward expression, Dygon set down the water cup. "I've no doubt," he said, forcing a knowing smile. "Like the rest of us, she enjoys her secrets."

The king grunted. "Oh, I doubt anyone enjoys secrets as much as you do, my friend," he said. Paeter gave the steward an affable slap on the shoulder. "Now, if you'll excuse me. I'm off to see my queen." Pushing past Dygon, the king picked up his traveling cloak and flung it about his shoulders, tying it off.

If the king went to the queen's chambers this moment, it was possible he would not find her there. It was possible E'lisea remained in the Midnight Court, shackled above that bed, naked and bloody, whimpering and begging for more, somehow deriving pleasure from such base treatment. Dygon fought back a twitch of his lips. But what could he do? *Oh, sister,* he lamented. Inside, he hated himself for his present helplessness.

"Get some sleep, Dygon," said Paeter, drawing the steward from his internal quandary.

The steward turned to watch the king open the door. *How can I?* He forced a sigh, then nodded. "You too, old friend," he said.

When the door shut again, Dygon hurriedly locked it then collapsed into his chair. Resting his chin on his hands, the king's steward wondered: Which of the queen's secrets would enrage her husband more? The magik or the pleasure? Would he find out in a matter of moments? Or had the queen returned to her chambers? *For your sake, sister, I hope you have.*

FOURTEENTH

DAWN STILL WAS far off and many pleasure-seekers, masked and unmasked alike, wandered the vermilion streets of the Midnight Court. Both fever and fear ever-building inside her, Niscene E'terrall clung desperately to the queen as the two women made their way toward the royal palace. She mumbled incoherencies under her breath but E'lisea either quieted her with whispered reassurances or else paid them no mind.

At nearly every turn, the queen stopped to cast a new cooling spell on Niscene. Yet, her head continued to burn. Intermittently, she also shivered, and strange visions soon blurred her eyesight. "He's coming for me!" she whispered, more to herself than to the queen. She glanced over her shoulder. Sometimes she thought she saw Ash'an Rah following close behind. Other times she sighted only shadows. But whenever she blinked, he was there – in the medial haze between eyes open and shut; his own flaming red eyes bored into her. *"You will do what must be done. You are Morad'ash."*

Each time the terrible voice spoke, Niscene shivered with fright and fever. At times she stumbled or tripped, but E'lisea would keep her from falling to the cobbled or brick streets.

"We are almost there, mistress," the queen whispered, gripping her hand all the tighter. "I promise."

The terrible voice of Ash'an Rah erupted again in Niscene's mind. *"Your life is forfeit!"* She moaned softly, unable to do much else. The Sense called to her through the fog of fever and paranoia, but she could not seize it. *Why?* she screamed on the inside. *Why is this happening? Why are you haunting me?* The shadowy vision of Ash'an Rah gave its usual reply: *"Do what must be done."*

"Nearly there," E'lisea whispered, kissing Niscene's

burning forehead. The kiss was cool, offering a temporary respite from her blurry vision and fiery mind. Lifting her head to the sky, Niscene noted that they had left the Midnight Court. The air no longer was weighted down by the thick red haze. Above, stars glowed white in the night sky, and the bright yellow moon hung over the palace.

Visible from all corners of the city, the royal palace, massive and glimmering even in the dark of night, loomed over Ramodin. Built into the side of the Mountain at the End of the World, the castle soared into the sky, its towers and spires and parapets stretching into the heavens like fingers, some even above the clouds and mist that shrouded the mountain peak farther up still. Lantern and torch light flickered in windows and balconies up and down its many steeples, giving the enormous edifice an even more ominous look.

Beneath the light of the full moon, the palace shimmered, its blue stone towers glistening like water. Staring at it through her temporary respite, Niscene felt small, insignificant. A feeling she despised. Instantly, anger flashed through her.

Niscene averted her eyes as she and the queen entered

the King's Square, which was adjacent to the palace. In the middle of the square sat a massive fountain of the gods, with ten marble figures posed in various positions. Water flowed and spewed from each statue pouring into the fountain's pool. The sound of the water, however, was drowned out by those who congregated at tables and tents which circled the fountain and dotted the rest of the King's Square. Vendors and merchants swooped and bowed and scraped at patrons and other few visitors to the Nighttime Market, some of whom Niscene noticed wore black masks like those of the Midnight Court.

As the hour was late, only a few dozen patrons wandered the market. When E'lisea and Niscene passed by, vendors and merchants shouted out extravagant descriptions of the items in their tents or on their tables to lure the ladies in for a possible sale. Love potions, silks from across the sea, plants brought all the way from the Endless Desert that never required water. Even bakers hawked what smelled like fresh-baked bread and pastries.

"Bloody vultures," the queen said through gritted teeth, leading Niscene around a crowd of merchants holding out their various wares. Ahead, at the west side of the square, Niscene saw a tall, forbidding iron gate. It stood between two thick stone walls that stretched high and encircled the palace.

E'lisea led them past the final row of merchants' tables and guided Niscene up the few steps to the gate. "Say nothing," she whispered to Niscene. "We're nearly inside."

An involuntary shiver shook Niscene, who bobbed her head up and down. The latest cooling spell had worn off and her paranoia soon reached fever pitch. Over her shoulder, she glanced at the market, her eyes scanning the crowd for the shadowy figure of Ash'an Rah. *He is coming for me,* she reminded herself. Again, she shivered, and tried desperately not to blink.

"Say nothing," the queen repeated. "Not a word."

Ahead, three guards stood outside the gate, laughing. But they stopped when one pointed in the women's direction.

One of the guards approached. "De'liah?" he asked, hopeful.

"Yes, Westin," said E'lisea without hesitation. She threw a quick, warning glance at Niscene, who felt the queen squeeze her hand then let it go. Somehow, Niscene managed to keep her balance; staring blurry-eyed at the queen, she protested. *Don't leave me,* she wanted to say. Her head burned and she felt a dark presence looming over her.

The guard relaxed when he heard the queen's voice. He looked back and waved at his two fellows. In her paranoid state, Niscene noticed their tense postures loosen. They returned to their chuckles.

"Back so soon?" the guard said, turning back to the women. He glanced at Niscene and grinned. "And with a friend?" The man's eyes looked her up and down, a curious and hungry glint in them. He frowned. "What's the matter with this one? Looks rather ill, she does."

"Oh, Westin, you're so astute," said E'lisea with a rather annoyingly high-pitched laugh. "She is indeed a very *special* friend." She tossed her hair back over her shoulders and pushed out her chest. The action drew the guard's eyes away from Niscene.

"Well, we've gotta keep a keen eye about things, you know," said the guard, nodding in the direction of the market.

"Oh, yes," said the queen. Again, she let out another irritatingly high-pitched laugh. "No one keeps a keener eye than you, dear Westin." E'lisea tilted her head in a coquettish way then extended a finger to give the man's nose a soft tap. His face split into a wide grin.

"But perhaps this time…" the queen stepped closer to the guard, gently pressing her breasts against his dinted armor, and running a hand over his face. "Perhaps…*this* time…you only saw *me* return?" E'lisea then turned her lips downward into a deep pout, and her eyes nearly doubled in size. "I'm not *really* supposed to bring *special* friends home with me. If the queen ever found out…"

"No," said the guard, stopping her with a hand. "We can't have that. *I* can't have that." Over his shoulder, he glanced up at the prodigious palace. He shook his head. "Let's get you back inside before the queen realizes you've been gone. No doubt she's fast asleep."

Despite her feverish and paranoid stupor, Niscene registered the guard's words. Her lips turned down into a strange, confused frown. Then, she felt the rumbling of a laugh rise up inside. But she then blinked and the laughter caught in her throat as the fiery vision of Ash'an Rah flashed in front of her. *"Do what must be done!"* Niscene's head swirled as the queen guided her up the steps to the gatehouse.

"Oh, she'll never suspect a thing," E'lisea said to the guard. With her free hand, she caressed the man's cheek, then walked her fingers down, over his armor and farther still. The man's face cracked into a fleshy, red grin before he regrettably gestured for the women to follow him to the gate.

E'lisea retracted her hand and followed. She turned to smile at Niscene, but her face paled. The queen whispered reassurances. "We're nearly there, mistress," she said. She squeezed Niscene's hand.

When they stepped up to the gate, the other two guards made no acknowledgement of the women. They seemed not to notice them at all; instead, they exchanged gossip and words about some lord or lady.

Moments later, the women were through the gate and in a courtyard. A stone pathway dead-ended at a sweeping staircase that led up to a columned landing. But instead of continuing in that direction, E'lisea led Niscene off the stone path behind some tall, naked trees into a garden of meticulously manicured rose bushes. The aroma of sweet roses and earthy moss filled the air.

If the queen had not led her directly to it, Niscene never would have found the door.

"A servants entrance," E'lisea whispered, answering the unasked question. Slipping a key from somewhere, the queen slipped it into the lock. A moment later, there was a click, then E'lisea pulled open the door. It made no sound.

The two women entered into a narrow corridor lined with sparsely placed lanterns, from which a dull, dim light emanated.

"I'm sorry, mistress," said the queen. "It's a long way up to my tower. I'd carry you if I could." She smiled, then kissed Niscene, who shivered at the sudden, temporary cooling of her mind.

"Come," said E'lisea, closing the door. "I know it is dark and you are ill, but we've only to climb to my tower. We'll take the steps one at a time. When we reach my rooms, I will…call on…the healer to help you."

Niscene's mind swirled as they walked through the flexuous, dimly lit passageways. Intermittent visions of Ash'an Rah continued to push her mind further into hysteria. Shadows danced along the cold, stone walls, mingling with fever-induced memories to recreate moments in her life she wished to forget.

Then, in a rare moment of clarity from her fever dreams, Niscene saw the queen ahead of her, hand gripped tightly around her own, helping her traverse the uneven stone steps that led up and up. Sweet E'lisea, who had shown her more kindness than anyone she could remember. The woman with the honeysuckle lips. *Must I kill you?* Niscene wanted to ask. *I cannot live without your kiss.* In the hazy light of the cold corridor, looking down at her, E'lisea met her eyes, and smiled.

Finally, after ascending one set of stairs that seemed to go on forever, the queen stopped in front of a door. She placed her ear to it for a moment. Then she opened it. The women walked out into a wide, high-ceilinged hallway. The ceiling was arched, with perfectly polished stone walls covered in paintings and portraits; undoubtedly priceless vases, heirlooms and other works of art lined the walls. A rich maroon carpet stretched across the floor fringed with gold. The hallway was wide enough for five people to walk side by side. Lanterns provided light enough to see and walk by. Through her mental haze, Niscene saw only opulence and excess. She felt small again, as she had when they approached the palace.

"Do you like it?" the queen asked, smiling at Niscene's agape face. "Far better accommodations than that dusty, creaky old pleasure house, yes?" She squeezed Niscene's hand then leaned in and kissed her on the cheek. "By the gods!" she said. "My chambers are just around the corner. Quickly! Your head is on fire!"

Hurriedly, she guided Niscene down the hall and turned a corner that dead-ended at a set of large double doors. As they approached, Niscene blinked and the visage of Ash'an Rah reappeared. *"Do what must be done."* She shivered as her eyes shot open. Her mind burned.

They stopped at the double doors long enough for the queen to unlock them. They entered a cool, darkened room. Just inside the door, the queen lit a small tallow candle. "Sit here, and–" Suddenly, the queen cried out: "Paeter!"

FIFTEENTH

SO TAKEN BY her fever visions, Niscene froze when she saw the tall figure rise from deeper in the room. Her breath caught in her throat. *Ash'an Rah! Here? I knew he was coming for me!* But, no. It was not the shadowy Hand of Death who stood before them. Rather, King Paeter, first of his name, and husband to E'lisea, walked toward them out of the depths of the darkened room.

"E'lisea!" he said. "Where have you been?" His voice was a deep, commanding baritone. A king's voice in every way. Niscene despised it immediately. In truth, there was nothing about Paeter, first of his name and king of the realm, Niscene enjoyed. Everything about him that E'lisea had shared flooded her mind. All the sordid details and secrets that she whispered in Niscene's only hours earlier replayed, like a list of grievances: he never understood her desires, he cared more for his crown than his queen. *"Men are such fools, you know. Kings more so."* Niscene recalled the pleasant sound of E'lisea's laugh when she had made her quip. How the queen had cupped her face and kissed her but then laughed again, its sound airy and melodious, like a spring breeze. It was a song Niscene found herself wishing to hear again; a song she was meant to silence forever.

Stunned, E'lisea said, "You are–"

"Home," the king finished, moving closer to grab the queen's hand. "Yes." The man's hands were large and rough; they swallowed E'lisea's. "I missed you. I thought–" But he did not share what it was he thought; the king's green eyes narrowed. "What is that on your face?" the king demanded. He touched one of his hands to the queen's black leather mask, touching it hesitantly. Then, violently, he ripped it from her face. E'lisea flinched as she raised a hand to feel her suddenly unmasked countenance. She stepped backward until her back pressed against the wall.

"This is one of those masks the bloody degenerates wear," the king said. He stared at the mask as though it were a vile thing. "The Midnight Court? Please, E'lisea, tell me you haven't..." He trailed off as he raised his eyes to look at her. "Tell me you..." His eyes widened and he shook his head, refusing to believe the thought that crossed his mind. "No," he said. "Tell me it's not true."

Pressed against the wall, E'lisea looked less like a queen and more like a little girl who faced punishment from her father. The light of the tallow candle illuminated her pale face, and her eyes darted from Niscene to the king. "M-my king," she said, stammering. "It is late, and—"

"Tell me!" the king shouted, throwing the mask across the room. It struck something in the darkness before falling to the carpeted floor. The king's expression hardened and he loomed over his queen like a nightmare.

E'lisea bowed her head, not meeting the man's intense gaze. "Paeter..." she whispered but trailed off. She began to quiver with fear, as though anticipating what came next: With a violent blow, the king struck her across the face. The queen cried out – not in pleasure, but fearful pain, dropping the candle. The tiny light winked out as the candle tumbled to the floor. The king struck her again and again, each blow eliciting more tears and anguish and despair.

Not five steps away, Niscene stood frozen, observing the abusive scene play out. In her feverish state, she saw not the king beating his queen, but her own brother striking her. *"'No' is not an option, Niscene,"* Login said in his emotionless voice. With each blow, she winced, a phantom throbbing running across her body, as if she received those strikes anew. She cowered, pleading with her brother, receiving only pain in response.

On the periphery, the Sense began to sing to her, to call to her, as though for the first time. Out of the corner of her consciousness, Niscene saw it, as always. Curious, she reached to seize it, to know its sweet power. At first low and brooding, the song of the Sense soon grew louder. The notes became dissonant and chaotic; discordant tones swirled in Niscene's mind. She blinked. In the median, Ash'an Rah's fiery eyes stared at her and his refrain echoed: *Do what must be done.*

Yes, she thought, as the Sense flowed into her. *What must be done.*

"You've been spending your nights in the Midnight

Court!" the king cried. He unleashed another violent blow against the queen. "Haven't you? Answer me!" The subsequent strike sent E'lisea to the floor. She began to weep.

When the king drew back his hand for his next blow, his arm froze in the air, barred by some invisible force. "What is this?" he asked, enraged. Wild-eyed, he looked about and his eyes fell on Niscene. "Who are you?" he demanded.

Without a word, Niscene, the sweetness of the Sense pulsing through her, struck. She began to whip him with air, forcing the king to teeter backward. He flailed against his seemingly invisible foe until he lost his footing and fell, hitting his head hard against the floor. He did not move.

The chaos of the Sense swirled within her like a winter storm. *Do what must be done. Yes,* she thought. She would do what must be done to save E'lisea. Such a fool as this did not deserve her. Niscene slowly approached the king, who lay unconscious on the floor. She had come to the city to kill a queen, but instead would kill a king.

Suddenly, the Sense began to waver, its haunting melody flickering in her mind. What was happening?

Niscene gripped tighter to the Sense but again some strange sensation threatened to loosen her hold. The Sense howled.

"No! Stop!" Niscene whirled around. Before her stood E'lisea, bruises on her face, blood on her lips, and outrage in her blue eyes. "Don't you *dare* touch him!" she hissed.

Stunned, Niscene stared at the other woman. "But, I was–" Her vision went white as the air struck her across the face. "E'lisea–" But the queen did not listen. She erupted, unleashing blow after blow against her. The Sense howled and cried out and Niscene clung to it. Anger quickly smothered her confusion and she fought back. With a swipe of her hand, she struck the queen, then deflected a blow. Then she attempted to lay a block on the other woman, separating her from the Sense. But E'lisea countered and pushed her over with a gust of air.

Niscene flew backward, crashing hard into a far wall. The impact knocked the air from her lungs and the Sense from her grip. As her body collapsed to the floor, she let out a whimper before the world went black.

Close to tears, E'lisea teetered near complete collapse. The only thing that kept her from falling to her knees was the Sense, which hummed softly. *Healing*, she thought. *I ought to heal myself.* But she remained standing, the Sense swirling within her, yet not wielding any magik or casting any spell. Instead, her tired mind tried to piece together the night, which had begun so well, but had taken a rather unexpected turn.

It all started when her brother had barged in, interrupting their session, frightening E'lisea out of her wits. A twinge of guilty annoyance twisted her insides. *Oh, brother, why could you not have left me be?*

Then her poor mistress suddenly burning up with fever on the street, her eyes and head darting back and forth as if being chased by one of the Morad'ash. E'lisea glimpsed in the direction of her unconscious mistress. Bringing her back to the palace had been a gambit, solid truth. And a sour one, at that, considering her present predicament. Of course, there had been no guarantees. There never were when dealing with whom it was she had hoped would help. E'lisea sighed.

Then, of course, there was the matter of her kingly husband's unexpected return.

With a heavy sigh, the queen staggered over to where Paeter lay, unconscious on the floor. "Oh, Paeter," she said, crouching beside the man. "You foolish, foolish man. Why did you return early? We could have avoided this whole sordid affair." She sighed. "Doubtless it is a painful realization," she whispered, slowly running a hand through the man's red locks. "Learning that your queen finds pleasure outside of your bed." One of the bruises beneath her eye throbbed, and she winced. *Painful, indeed.* "But you'll learn to accept it. Because gods know I won't stop." Her lips curled upward into a mischievous grin. "Of course, even if you don't…" Breathing in deeply, E'lisea began to wield her magik; the Sense sang a familiar melody. Sweet and pleasant, it imbued the queen with a renewed sense of energy. "I certainly won't mind your beatings."

She leaned in so her face was next to the king's. Licking her lips, she said, "You may not know this, my love, but I find pain *incredibly* pleasurable." To stifle a laugh forming in her belly, she kissed Paeter, leaving behind a spot of blood on his upper lip. "After all," she whispered. "I've still a secret that would offend you far more than any sexual dalliance."

With a long, languorous stretch, E'lisea rose from her position on the floor. Thrusting her arms into the air and tossing back her head, she began to work the healing spell. Her body began to tingle then suddenly it struck her: *I cannot heal myself. Not this time.* Not if she wished to keep *that* secret from him. There truly was no telling what Paeter would do were he to learn that she could hear the Sense, that she could wield magik. If he ever found that out, she would never be able to fulfill her obligation to protect him, annoyance that it was.

"Well, shit," E'lisea said aloud. Bracing herself, she let go the Sense. The sudden emptiness still brought tears to her eyes, even after all these years. She wiped them away, wincing through the bruises and swollen lip. She wondered how long it would take for her face to heal naturally. Or when she again would be able to steal away to the Midnight Court. Nothing about this night was turning out to be easy.

And what to do about her mistress? The strange woman had not budged since E'lisea blasted her across the room. She stepped past Paeter and crouched down next to her. What had the woman been thinking, attacking the king as she did? Had she so quickly forgotten how much E'lisea craved the pleasure of pain? Had she really believed all that foolishness about fearing for her life? *As if I would ever fear any man, king or not,* she mused.

"I didn't want us to fight," the queen said, crouching next to the unconscious woman. "I meant what I said. I would fuck you every night if I could." Her lips twisted into a wry grin, then she sighed. "I was hoping to keep you around a bit longer. You truly are remarkable, mistress."

It was true. Never had she experienced a pleasure mistress who could hear the Sense – and wield it in such a wild, violent fashion. The queen's body tingled as she thought of the painful pleasures she had received over the past week.

"I even saved you from those boorish rapers, and nursed you back to health in that inn for two nights." E'lisea shook her head as if in disbelief. "You really should not have attacked Paeter. Fool, he may be, but he's far more important than you. Of course, I'm perhaps the bigger fool."

That was the way of things sometimes. It's not as if the queen had not fallen for her mistresses before. Several, in fact, she had fucked in her own bed. Right under Paeter's nose.

Once more, she embraced the Sense, taking a brief moment to relish the intoxicating power as it flooded into her. Taking a deep breath, E'lisea extended a hand and touched the left side of the woman's chest.

As the Sense pulsed through her, singing a low, dark melody, the queen whispered a few words, then blinked. A whole new world appeared before her. The pleasure mistress still lay in front of her, but instead of her olive skin, E'lisea saw deeper – beneath the skin. The inner workings of the woman's body flowed, worked, and pulsed, albeit slowly. Like a strange, otherworldly portrait, the queen saw veins and muscles, bones and organs. Blood flowed this way and that, the lungs expanded and deflated. The heart pulsed.

Viewing the interior workings of the body was a magik all its own, a fascinating creation of the Maker E'lisea wished to observe in greater detail. Had she the time. Which, at this moment, she did not.

She narrowed in on the heart. The reddish mass that sat just below the left breast, signaling life with its soft, steady beat.

Keeping her one hand on the unconscious woman's chest, E'lisea raised her other one and, reaching out, grabbed hold of the heart – and squeezed. Immediately, the woman's body began to convulse; short, rapid gasps escaped her lips.

"I am sorry, mistress," said the queen.

Sleep was an escape for Niscene E'terrall. Unconscious, her mind was silent and her head cooled. No more fever. No more questions. No more fear or anger. Just the comfort of a dreamless sleep.

However, like the approaching dawn, Niscene's mind slowly began to stir. Consciousness returned and a dull ache that stretched from her head down through her feet registered, followed by a rush of memory: She lay upon the floor in the queen's chambers; the king had been beating her mercilessly. *I attacked him, then she attacked me.* Niscene wanted to dwell on that thought, despite the pain it caused deep inside her. But she was not afforded such a luxury, because without warning a suffocating pain shattered her stream of awakening thought – like someone stood over her smothering her heart with a vice. Niscene gasped for air, finding it nearly impossible to breathe. Her eyes shot open and she saw E'lisea. The queen stood over her, a hand pressed firmly against Niscene's chest, and a hardened look on her beautiful face.

"Don't fight it, mistress," said the queen. "It will all be over soon."

But deep within her, a primal desire roared to life. Niscene wanted nothing more than to fight, to live. Desperately, she reached out for the Sense, which whistled like a raging wind, but could not seize it. No matter how close she came to grabbing hold of it, the Sense was just out of reach. *No!* she cried out in her mind. *Not again!*

Panic began to set in as Niscene stared, wide-eyed, at E'lisea. The queen regarded her with a knowing smile and hard, blue eyes. "I truly am sorry, mistress," said the queen in a voice as cold as ice.

No! Gods, no! Niscene was unsure whether she managed to spit out the words or if they were only in her mind. Her breath rapidly dissipated, yet still she tried to thrash and flail. She lashed out with arms and legs, hoping to land a kick or scratch. But it was all in vain. E'lisea easily brushed aside all such attempts with small bursts of air.

"You have fire, mistress," said the queen. "It is a pity you have to die."

The grip around Niscene's heart tightened, and her vision flashed between white and black and other colors as she stared in strange horror at the woman whom she had come to love slowly killing her. Suddenly, her head began to burn and the familiar, all-consuming voice of Ash'an Rah crashed through her skull: *"Do what must be done!"*

This woman – this queen whom she had grown to love, who even saved her life – how had it come that she now loomed over her, hand twisted around Niscene's heart, squeezing the the very life out of it? Among the chaos unfolding in her mind – the Sense howling and the haunting, flaming vision of Ash'an Rah – Niscene heard the one voice she despised above all others. The voice that set her on a lifetime of pain and despair and darkness. *"Nobody loves you, Niscene,"* her brother, Login, whispered in his flat, emotionless tone. *"Nobody ever will."*

He was right.

Fueled by panic, fear, and something else she could not explain, Niscene exploded with fury and rage, clawing and lashing out for the Sense. Still, it evaded her, and large circles of yellow light began to pop to life in front of her eyes. She gritted her teeth and blinked them away. Her inner fire continued to burn. *You are strong, my queen. But – I – am – stronger!*

Just as she choked out her final breath and the world began to swirl together into a thousand fading colors, Niscene heard the queen cry out. Then, the Sense flooded into her like water raging out from behind a broken dam. Niscene seized it all, every last bit of power she could grab. Her mind still dizzy from near-death and fever pitch, she took hold of every ounce of magik and Sense she saw and felt. Reaching farther and deeper than ever she had before, Niscene snatched and clawed, until a strange melody filled her ears, commingling with the familiar song she knew so well. The discordant melodies swirled and swung in her mind, growing louder till they nearly deafened her.

Above the sweet chaotic notes of the music playing, pulsing all around her, Niscene heard the queen cry one word: "No!"

Suddenly, her vision split and Niscene saw both E'lisea and herself, as though looking through each set of eyes. The queen was frightened; she saw it in her eyes but also sensed it – *knew* it for true. With a thought, Niscene focused on the queen's hand gripped around her heart and loosened it.

"Maker's mercy!" E'lisea whimpered. "Paeter!"

"That bloody *d'ongrata* won't save you now," said Niscene. Her voice, low and hard, echoed in her ears and the queen's.

Filled with twice the power of the Sense, Niscene allowed rage to guide her. Through E'lisea's eyes she saw the inner workings of her body; holding tightly to the woman's Sense, she knew easily what to do though never before had she worked such magik. With just a thought, she, too, saw the insides of the queen's body: the chaotic mess of muscles and veins and organs all tense and working rapidly under distress. The heart was easy to see.

"Please!" the queen whispered. "Don't! I'm so–" E'lisea's words cut off as Niscene clutched the woman's heart. The song of the *Sei'na* clanged and crashed as it morphed into one terrible, haunting, merciless melody.

"Oh, gods! No!" the queen gasped. Niscene squeezed harder, literally smothering the life out of the woman – doing what must be done. *From this day to my last I shall hold the world's fate in my hands,* she recited in her mind.

The queen began to toss and turn gasping for one last breath, trying in vain to free herself and pull away from Niscene's invisible grip.

I am a Bringer of Chaos. I am a Servant of the Lady of Death.

"Maker's mercy!" E'lisea whispered. Plea–!'"

But she did not finish. The beating of the queen's heart gave one final spasm then ceased. E'lisea's convulsions and panicky movement halted. Her body fell limp, falling with a hard thud against the carpeted floor.

Niscene breathed the final line of her creed: "I am Morad'ash."

Sixteenth

Silence fell across the room.

"E'lisea?" Niscene murmured, as if awakening from a dream.

The deed done – how suddenly it all had happened – she let go of the Sense, allowing the sweet storm of chaos to seep out, back to the fringes of her mind. She winced at the abrupt emptiness; it rose up to meet her, as if to swallow her whole. But, as always, it passed. Though the dread she felt did not. Niscene's lips quivered. She blinked and fixed her onyx eyes upon the queen's body, lying on the floor. Unmoving. Lifeless. Dead. Wide, glazed-over blue eyes stared up at her. E'lisea's velvet lips were frozen in mid-cry, but made no sound. They never would again.

"What have I done?" Niscene moaned, falling to her knees beside the body of her lover. Seizing the Sense, she gently caressed and stroked the queen's face, muttering words and spells, enchantments and intercessions into the silence of the room. Already, the warmth of E'lisea's cheeks was fading.

A sharp and powerful ache pierced Niscene right in the chest, as if an assassin suddenly had thrust a blade straight into her heart. Like a poison, the ache spread and she began to shake uncontrollably as the realization settled in.

"Oh, gods!" she cried, pressing her hands to her face. She rocked back and forth, feeling her insides twist and coil into knots. "My sweet queen! What have I done?" she bemoaned. The response came cold and clear, sending a shiver across her soul: *What had to be done.*

Still, the tears came, and through tiny gasps and moans, Niscene pulled E'lisea's body into her arms. With the tenderness of a lover, she swayed back and forth, attempting to wake her. To coax her back to life. The queen stared up at her with dead, accusatory eyes that made Niscene's skin crawl. With a shaky hand, she reached out and closed them. She whispered the woman's name over and over: "E'lisea…E'lisea…E'lisea…"

When her voice ran out, Niscene traced her fingers across the queen's dead lips. Soft as velvet and nearly as sweet as the Sense, the woman's lips had intoxicated her. Like a drug, she came to need them. Soft and wet, delicate, always with a hint of mischief and honeysuckle, the queen's kisses were unlike anything Niscene had ever before experienced. A surprise bloom of high summer fire flowers amid a blanket of midwinter snow.

Pursing her lips, Niscene leaned down, yearning for one more kiss from the queen. But her anticipation was met with bitter disappointment. E'lisea's lips were cold. So cold. Niscene turned her head and came cheek to cheek with the dead queen. She squeezed shut her eyes as tears stung at them once more. Again finding her voice, she said, "Forgive me."

Across the room, the king stirred.

Niscene froze. So overtaken by her sorrow, she had forgotten about King Paeter. Lifting her head, she squinted through the darkness toward the outline of the man lying in a mess upon the floor. A soft groan escaped his lips and he murmured something indecipherable. He began to rouse from his unconsciousness. First, a hand touched to his head then he bent a knee and pressed a foot into the floor.

"E'lisea," he murmured. What ha–"

Acting quickly and from instinct, Niscene seized the Sense and slowly tugged at the air floating around the king. Instantly, he yawned. His knee stretched out lengthwise along the floor and he smacked his lips as exhausted old men do. He muttered tired words under his breath and relaxed into a peaceful sleep.

By thinning out the air around him just enough, Niscene was confident the king would sleep through the rest of the night. Of course, how long that might be, only the gods knew. Since leaving the Midnight Court, Niscene had lost track of all time. Dawn could be still hours away or about to break. Regardless, as she watched the king's chest rise up and down from across the room, she knew it was past time to leave. *And to the shadows shall I return.*

She carried the queen to her bed. A four-poster made of aged black oak, Niscene had never seen a bed so large.

The mattress was soft, with silk sheets and down pillows. A thick, velvet curtain draped across all sides of it, likely to aid in blocking out the sun and moon while the queen slept. At that moment, the moon cast a yellowish glow into the bed chamber, giving E'lisea's pale, cold face a more sickly complexion.

As she laid the queen upon the bed, Niscene dwelled on what might have been. *"I would fuck you every night if I could."* E'lisea's words cut through her heart.

"Too late," Niscene muttered, turning from the lifeless body.

Dealing with the king proved another matter entirely. Where E'lisea was dead, her kingly husband merely slept, and lay sprawled on the floor, at that. He could not stay there. It would raise too many questions once day came. "I shall leave no trace or memory of my presence," Niscene whispered as she loomed over the slumbering monarch. What to do, then?

In the end, though it pained her beyond comprehension, she made use of the Sense to place the man in bed beside his dead queen. *Let him wake to the sorrow he himself caused.* After all, the bastard king deserved sorrow

– and far worse. If he had not been waiting in the queen's chambers, E'lisea still would be alive. And she and Niscene would be together beneath the silken sheets, making love by the light of the full moon.

"*You* killed her," Niscene whispered. "Not I." *I loved her.*

Like an assassin, she loomed over the king, his chest rising and falling with the slow, steady breaths of deep sleep, blissfully unaware that his life was in any danger. The Sense swirled and pulsed throughout her. Its haunting melody filled her ears, calling to her. Niscene's hands hovered over the man, her fingers twitching as they descended. *Yes,* she reflected. *You deserve to die.* Slowly, she lowered her hands, drawing them closer to the king's thick neck. *I am a Bringer of Chaos. I am a Servant of the Lady of Death.* When her fingers were but a hair's breadth above the man's neck, she whispered: "I am Morad'ash."

Just then, a soft rapping stabbed at the haunting silence. Hovering over the king, Niscene tensed. Swallowing a curse, she whipped her head around in the direction of the noise. She narrowed her onyx eyes as the rapping came again, louder this time, followed by a muffled, anxious voice. Beside her, the king mumbled and began to rouse from his sleep.

Frantically, Niscene dropped to the cold floor. With the king stirring above her, she had no time to hide anywhere but beneath the bed. She scuttled underneath as the king sat up, mumbling and muttering under his breath. Within her, the Sense howled, and Niscene's heart pounded in her chest, threatening to break out. She willed herself to silence.

The rapping came again and the king murmured something Niscene could not make out.

Above her, Niscene heard the bed creak as the king moved. A moment later, he lifted himself out of the bed and plodded tiredly to the door. From her hiding place, Niscene heard the lock click, then watched as the king pulled open the doors.

"Father?" came the confused voice of a young girl. In the doorway she stood, holding a lantern in one hand that gave off a soft, flickering light.

"Penaelope?" the king said, equally confused. "What in the name of Lady Death are you doing out of bed?" He glanced over his shoulder and Niscene's heart caught in her throat. She swore the man was staring right at her. But her fears were unfounded when he shook his head and turned back to his daughter in the doorway. "It is late, child," he said in a lowered voice. "And walking all the way up here?"

"You're home early," the girl said, though she sounded not at all surprised or interested in the king's presence. Rather, she lifted her lantern and peered past her father, at the bed behind him. Again, Niscene went rigid. She most certainly would be discovered. Doubtless, the princess saw her. But it was not so. "Is Mother...?" the girl's question trailed off. Her voice was shaky.

"She is sleeping, child," the king answered matter-of-factly. He stepped aside to gesture to the bed. "And quite soundly. I returned early and came to be with her. What is the matter?"

From her vantage, Niscene could see the girl – Princess Penaelope, daughter to the king and queen. The girl was clearly anxious. By the light of her lantern, Penaelope's face appeared pale and tired. Finally, her expression relaxed and she nodded. Lowering her light, she said, "Just bad dreams."

"Oh, child," the king said, pulling his daughter into a

hug. "I truly am sorry. I know they may seem real, but dreams cannot hurt us."

Penaelope nodded again. "I know," she said.

"Very good," said the king. "Now, come. It is late. Very nearly dawn, no doubt, and you ought to get back to sleep. I shall accompany you." He placed a hand on his daughter's shoulder and started to guide her back out the door.

"Yes, Father," the princess said, acquiescing.

When the door shut behind the king and princess, silence again fell over the darkened room. Still, Niscene did not move. She half expected the door to reopen at any moment and the king to return. Minutes passed and the door remained shut. She wondered how far away the girl's room was from the Tower of the Queen. How long would it take for the king to return? Would he return? What was she waiting for? *He deserves to die*, she reminded herself. *Yes. But perhaps not this night.*

Niscene knew the time had come to flee the palace, to flee the city, and leave behind this whole sordid affair. "I've done what I came to do," she said in the darkness beneath the bed. *And to the shadows shall I return.* Touching a hand to her face, Niscene dried her eyes.

As she crawled out from underneath the bed, her hand brushed over something that felt like lace and leather: E'lisea's mask. Somehow it had ended up beneath the bed after the king had thrown it across the room. Something stirred within her and Niscene gripped it tightly. When she finally managed to free herself from her hiding place, she stood and tied it around her face.

One last time, she stood beside the queen's lifeless body. Niscene could feel the death on the woman. "Forgive me," she whispered as she drew nearer. She licked her lips, expectantly. Then Niscene stole one final kiss. The dead woman's lips were ice cold. "Farewell, my queen."

Without looking back, Niscene silently slipped out the door into the expansive corridor. Lanterns flickered along the walls, giving light enough to see one's way. All was silent save the whispered flickering of the lanterns' magikal flames. Sticking to the shadows, Niscene sneaked along the stone wall, pausing every few feet to listen.

At the corner, she stopped to assess what lay around it. Again, only a handful of lanterns provided any light with which to see. Hazy though it was, Niscene saw what she searched for: the servants' passage she and E'lisea used to enter the palace unseen. Though racked by fever when they traversed it, Niscene recalled the direction they had come: up. To escape, she simply must descend.

She heard and saw nothing around the corner. The only sound was the ever-present call of the Sense, whose song, though familiar, had developed a strangeness about it. Steeling herself, Niscene stepped out from the shadows and glided across the hall, her breath catching in her throat. Once on the other side, she threw herself against the stone wall, shrouded in shadow. Her heart pounded in her chest as she let out her breath.

Half a heart beat later, Niscene ducked into the servants' passage and shut the door behind her. Goose flesh rose up on her skin and she shivered. A winter-like chill hung over the hazy passageway. *Move,* Niscene urged herself. That was all that mattered. *Escape.*

Silent as Death Herself, she descended the stone steps one at a time, feeling her fingers along the frigid wall to keep from tripping or falling down. Her hands quickly grew numb from the bitter chill and she had to stop to blow warm air into them.

Farther down, Niscene stepped, never passing another living soul, completely unaware of how much time passed or how soon dawn might break – if it had not already. The passage twisted and turned, and she stumbled upon random doors and other corridors and stairwells.

At one point, Niscene thought she heard footsteps behind her, almost matching hers step for step. Instantly, she seized the Sense and froze. With her sharpened senses, she listened closely, willing herself not to breathe, to remain as quiet as Ash'a.

But nothing – nor anyone – did she hear.

Cursing herself for her foolishness, Niscene let go of the Sense and resumed her descent.

She eventually reached a long, empty passage that dead-ended at a door. It opened easily and Niscene stepped out into the warm spring night. A shiver racked her body as it adjusted to the change in temperature. The warm late-night air was welcome relief after the stale, bone-chilling air of the labyrinthine servants' passageway.

A soft breeze whispered by, softly rustling the trees and bushes nearby, drawing out another shiver from Niscene. The scent of grass and roses filled her nostrils.

Dawn had not yet come, though by the looks of the moon, which hung low in the eastern horizon, it was near.

A wave of exhaustion suddenly rolled over her and her mouth twisted into a yawn. Shaking it off, Niscene rubbed her eyes. *Not yet*, she told herself. *Almost, but not yet.*

Cautiously, she made her way through the garden, stepping softly so not to draw unwanted attention from anyone who also may be enjoying a late-night or early morning stroll through the grove of rose bushes. Her caution proved unnecessary. As in the servants' passage, she neither passed nor heard another living soul while walking the garden. Not until she reached the garden's edge. When she did, Niscene stifled a curse. Not 50 feet away was the main gate, three guards' backs to her. Beyond, the few remaining sounds and lights of the Nighttime Market could be heard. Like the Sense, they teased and stung. Escape – freedom – was so close, yet Niscene stood frozen in the shadows of the rose garden.

That familiar twinge of fear crept up her spine. How to get past the guards? Had she come this far only to be trapped behind the palace gates?

At her sides, she balled her hands into fists attempting

to keep from lashing out. Then the Sense called to her, whispering its seductive song. *What a fool I am!* she scolded herself. She heard the Sense. With magik at her disposal, she would not be trapped by a trio of boorish gate guards. Nor trapped by anyone else. Reaching out to the edges of her consciousness, Niscene seized the Sense. Its power flowed through her. "Oh, yes," she said aloud, and laughed.

Almost immediately, the guards at the gate turned in unison to look right at her. Two of them stepped toward her, hands on hilts. "Hello? Who goes there?" asked one. In response, Niscene waved her hand, and the guards stopped. They looked about, confused. They even stared right at her but did not see her. A smile tugging at her lips, Niscene strode out of the garden, across the stone path, and right past the guards through the main gate. None saw her.

"What was it?" asked the guard who had stayed at the gate.

"Nothing," shrugged one of his comrades.

"Gods be good, I don't know!" exclaimed the other. "Thought I saw *something* there." He shook his head and rubbed his eyes. "But I suppose it was only shadows and wind." He shrugged. "It has been a long night."

The third guard chuckled and fell into razzing his fellows about ghosts and being afraid of the dark. All the while, Niscene E'terrall slipped away into the Nighttime Market, disappearing amongst the few remaining merchants, tinkers and late-night denizens who loitered about just before sunrise. But she paid them no mind as she passed. Now gone from the palace, her heart and mind were free to once more dwell on sorrowful things.

SEVENTEENTH

NOT LONG AFTER, Dygon's eyes shot open at the sound of knocking.

A quick glance at the window told him it was not that long after dawn; the first sliver of western sun beamed over the top of the mountain and began to push away the shadow of night. When the knocking came again, Dygon stood, rubbed his eyes, and went to open the door.

Standing in his doorway was his niece, Penaelope, the First Princess. The red-haired girl's blue eyes were wet and red. Her lips quivered. Fresh tears began streaming down the girl's face as soon as she saw her uncle.

His guard immediately up, Dygon knelt in front of her. Despite his years of practice and training, he felt his heart twist into knots. "What is it, Penaelope?" he asked. The princess began to shake and her uncle rested both hands on her shoulders to steady her.

When she managed to push out the words, Dygon pulled her close into a fierce hug. "Maker's mercy!" he gasped.

E'lisea appeared to be in a peaceful sleep. Her curious blue eyes were shut and her strawberry blonde curls fell about her porcelain face.

Hands at his sides, Dygon stood next to King Paeter, who knelt at the bedside, his dead queen's hands in his own.

"A Philosopher is on the way," Dygon said.

"Her hands," the king said, his voice hoarse with emotion. "They are so, so cold."

She died sometime in the night. That was what the king said. But how? Or from what? Penaelope had come seeking comfort for a nightmare and Paeter accompanied her back to her rooms. Or so Paeter said. Of course, the princess confirmed the story. And Dygon was fairly certain she had had nothing to do with her mother's death. Still, he would investigate further.

When Paeter returned – or so he said – he leaned in for a kiss but found E'lisea's lips to be ice cold.

Loyal though he was, Dygon was skeptical of the king's story. Then again, Paeter was no play actor; the agony on his face and sorrow racking his body could not possibly be feigned. Dygon did not want to believe Paeter would have harmed the queen, but when pressed for details from earlier in the evening, the king offered none. "I...I do not know," he had said with haunted eyes.

So, much to his frustration, and until he knew for certain, the steward could not dismiss the possibility that the king might somehow have done something to the queen.

Allowing the tiniest frown to touch his lips, Dygon examined his sister's lifeless body. If the king had murdered the queen, how had he done so? There was not a mark on her. Dygon scanned his sister's upper body but saw no visible sign of struggle such as choke marks or slit of the throat. He saw no visible sign of anything other than peaceful repose. By all appearances, Lady Death truly had escorted E'lisea away in her sleep.

But it makes no sense, Dygon mused. Days shy of her thirtieth year, the queen was in perfect health. At least she had appeared to be – when last he saw her.

Unconsciously, the steward raised a hand to his cheek to the spot where his sister had both hurt and healed him. Had she been hiding another secret? An illness? Perhaps manifested from years of wielding magik and hearing the Sense? Dygon clenched his teeth. He knew a great deal about a great many things, but sorcery, spellwork, enchantments, the Sense? The workings of magik remained a troubling mystery to him. *We all have too many bloody secrets.*

The sound of the opening door drew him from his thoughts. Over his shoulder, Dygon saw an old, white-haired man in blue robes seemingly float into the room. His robes appeared to shimmer with each step. The gaunt old man wore a faraway look on his pale, serene face; his hair was long, past his shoulders, and pulled into a meticulously braided ponytail that trailed down his back. Yet his face was perfectly shorn and free of beard or stubble. His hands were hidden in the sleeves of his robes, held in front of his chest.

Dygon turned and offered the slightest of nods to the visitor. He then gently placed a hand on the king's shoulder. "Your majesty," he said. "Philosopher Xanis is here."

Paeter did not immediately move or even acknowledge what Dygon had said. He remained seated by the bed, sad eyes fixed on his dead queen. After an extended moment, he sighed wearily then gently placed E'lisea's hands on her chest. Though sorrowful, he managed a scowl for the Philosopher.

"Your majesty," said Philosopher Xanis. His voice possessed the ethereal quality of all those trained in the Court of Servants. It sounded as though he spoke from someplace far away, another realm of otherworldly beings. The Philosopher offered the slightest of bows for the king – a mere courtesy, really. It was not lost on Paeter, who showed no such reciprocity. He merely spoke in a clipped tone. "Xanis."

"My deepest sympathies," Philosopher Xanis said, either ignoring or missing the blatant disregard the king showed him. "The queen was dear to all of us." He tilted his head to peer around Paeter and squinted his faraway eyes. "I have come to verify before sending up the white smoke."

Dygon stifled a derisive snort. Like the king, the steward was not fond of Philosophers – or their role in the kingdom.

With a gesture, the king stepped aside for the Philosopher to step beside the bed. The robed man did so and immediately frowned. With shaky hands, he touched E'lisea's forehead then moved down over her face, neck, and the rest of her body. Dygon glanced at the king, who looked ready to retch. Likely the sight of the Philosopher touching E'lisea, dead or not, made him ill.

"May the Maker's mercy be ever on our dear queen's soul," Philosopher Xanis said after a few more moments of examination. "May the earthly gods protect her on her journey to the Higher Realm."

"That's all you have to say?" the king asked through clenched teeth. "What of how she died?"

The white-haired man regarded the king with grey eyes. "It is unclear, your majesty," he said, his voice a distant breeze. "By all accounts she was a healthy young woman."

"She *is* healthy," Paeter said, slamming a fist against one of the bed posts. The massive bed rattled but Xanis was not. Despite a kingly glare that would have had any commoner or lord quaking in his boots, the Philosopher merely blinked. Those of the Court of Servants were not so easily bullied, Dygon knew.

"I am truly sorry, your majesty," Philosopher Xanis said, ignoring the king's attempt at intimidation. Dygon doubted the man's sentiments. "The queen is dead."

Like a bowman's arrow, those four words pierced the king. Dygon saw the defiance flicker in Paeter's face. His shoulders slumped and he gave a slight nod.

"Thank you, Philosopher," the king said flatly.

"I live to serve the realm, your majesty," Philosopher Xanis said, offering another perfunctory bow. "The white smoke shall be sent up within the hour. The Speakers shall be sent to prepare the body for burial. Funeral arrangements must be made."

With a wave, the king brushed aside the Philosopher's words. "Yes, yes," he said. Without another word, he turned his back on the old man to resume his vigil beside his dead queen. "Now, leave me to my mourning."

The Philosopher muttered a quick prayer before departing. With a keen eye, Dygon watched him go. With a Philosopher's confirmation, the rest of the city would soon know the news. The rumors and gossip would then begin. But what will they whisper in the taverns and common rooms throughout Ramodin? By all accounts, E'lisea was beloved by the city and its people. *But gossip always spreads*, Dygon reminded himself. *People can't help but whisper.* He knew that better than most. *But what will they say?*

The steward looked over the king's shoulder at the queen's pale face. *How did you die, sweet sister?*

Mere hours earlier, he had seen her alive. Yet, here she lay, dead with not a mark on her. Even a Philosopher's examination uncovered nothing untoward or suspicious. *How did you die, E'lisea?*

Had she harbored some secret illness? Was that what precipitated her sudden forays into the Midnight Court? Did she know her time was limited? The steward frowned at the king, on the ground in front of him. Had Paeter spoken the truth of what happened? Or had he discovered her just returning from the Midnight Court and gone mad with rage? *Too many damned questions!* Dygon despised nothing more than questions.

The king muttered something under his breath, then leaned in and gently kissed the forever slumbering woman on her forehead. "Cold," Paeter said. He then pressed his own forehead to E'lisea's and wept. "So very cold."

Dygon had never seen his friend and king so distraught. A memory, so rich and vivid a scene it could have played out that very moment, flickered in Dygon's mind. A pair of lovers fawning and cooing over each other before one is violently ripped away from the other's arms. One is beaten to death, the other sent far away and forgotten. Dygon turned his face away to avoid the painful memory. Despite his suspicions, he understood the king's apparent grief.

"Please, Dygon." The steward blinked at the sound of his name. He met Paeter's hollow green eyes. "Please... leave us. She was your sister, I know, but..." The king trailed off before falling into a fit of tears. He lifted E'lisea's cold, lifeless hand to his forehead again and wept silently.

Dygon opened his mouth to speak but decided against it. *Mourn for your queen, my friend.* He placed a comforting hand on the king's shoulder, then turned to leave.

May the Maker's mercy be upon your soul. Dygon would have an opportunity to mourn his sister's death. But not until he found some answers. *How did you die, sweet sister?*

EIGHTEENTH

AT FIRST, THE people of Ramodin did not notice the white smoke twisting its way out of the temple and into the early spring sky. Such an occurrence had not been seen in a good 10 years; it was an even rarer happening prior to then. People went about their early morning rituals of opening shops, dusting out rugs, collecting laundry, and walking the streets to the market.

Meanwhile, the smoke twisted and twirled, continuing its ascension into the morning, rapidly forming a rather thick unnatural cloud that soon covered the city. Smoke billowed and moved for several more moments before

Niscene E'terrall finally heard someone let out a shout. Lifting her tea to her lips, Niscene watched, attempting a casual detachment, as up and down the street, all activity paused whilst minds registered what they saw; heads craned and twisted to gain a better view. A myriad fingers jabbed at the sky. Then the chaotic aftermath began.

"What has happened?" asked a merchant running from his shop. His jaw dropped when he saw the smoke.

"Maker's mercy! The queen – dead?" a carriage driver shouted, halting his horses to stare dumbfounded into the sky. His horses snorted as though also shaken by the news, stomping at the cobbles along the street.

As the white smoke billowed and wafted into the air, city folk turned to city folk, hugging, praying, shouting, swearing, gasping. Some fainted at the sudden shock. Others wailed and moaned in grief. A group of washerwomen dropped their loads and ran down the street shouting something about the temple. A pair of goodwives fell into conspiratorial whispering – speculating, questioning, exchanging theories, gossiping as goodwives do.

Sitting at an outside cafe table, a soft spring breeze

blowing through her auburn hair, Niscene sipped tea and blended in, unnoticed.

So, they finally had discovered E'lisea's dead body. Doubtless, confusion reigned in the palace. After all, how could a healthy woman, not quite to her thirtieth year, suddenly die in her sleep? Niscene sighed into her tea cup. How, indeed. She took a sip, ignoring the twinge that cut at her insides.

Upon leaving the palace, Niscene had roamed the city streets, numb and alone and uncertain of where to go. With her task complete, she knew not what to do next. Though exhausted from the weight of the full moon and all that had occurred beneath it, she decided against returning to the Pleasure's Respite for fear of dreaming new dreams and dwelling on the gnawing in her chest. Instead, she wandered through Ramodin, clinging to the Sense and the succor it provided; its haunting melody was a numbing distraction from the sorrow that ate at her heart.

From the King's Square, she had wandered north past darkened taverns, as well as quiet inns and shops, then headed east toward the Midnight Court. There she came across a pair of drunken fools fucking in an alleyway. The man had the woman pressed up against the back wall, her skirt hiked up and her legs wrapped taut around his waist. He heaved and huffed and grunted whilst the girl moaned loudly and repeatedly shouted, "Yes! Yes! Yes! Gods, yes!"

Watching them, something possessed Niscene and she lashed out. The man's grunting turned to howls of pain and the woman's moans became shrieks of terror. In the end, Niscene left them in the alley in a shared pool of blood.

She spent the rest of the night wandering aimlessly south. She stumbled upon a forgotten line of laundry and stole a blouse and skirt in which to change, setting fire to her existing attire. Niscene then decided to wait until the main gate opened at dawn to avoid raising suspicion of a late-night departure. But when the first beams of sun peeked over the top of the mountain, she changed her mind, resolving to wait until she saw the smoke in the sky before leaving the city.

And now she saw it. As did everyone else. Still, Niscene lingered. Behind her lay the main gate. If she had a pebble to toss, she likely could hit the bloody thing or one of the dozens of pilgrims, farmers, tinkers, or merchants already converging on the capital. But all she had was a small money purse she had lifted from the drunk lovers she killed, and her cup of tea, which she lifted to her lips once again. The white smoke continued pouring out of the temple in the distance, pushing the cloud farther out into the sky. Another few minutes and it would expand enough to mix with the perennial grey clouds that shrouded the mountain peak and the highest towers of the palace.

"My lady?" The Sense ceased its soft singing and howled in annoyance at the sudden interruption. Niscene shared its sentiment. Scowling, she turned to find a nervous-looking young man standing next to her.

Not much younger than Niscene herself, the young man fidgeted with his hands as if he were pulling something apart. He stared at her with an anxious look in his soft blue eyes, and his fair hair blew softly in the morning breeze. He wore a fine suit of green and blue, with a brocaded pattern along the sleeves, but surely was no lordling; he lacked the haughtiness.

Why the fidgety fool had spoken to her, Niscene had not the slightest inclination. But she was in no mood to entertain such idiocy. Not ever. But least of all this morning.

Lowering her cup to the table, Niscene narrowed her onyx eyes and pursed her lips. "If you value your life, boy," she said, "I suggest you walk away." She arched an eyebrow and took another sip of tea. "Now."

The young man flinched as if the word stabbed him, but still failed to move. He swallowed then licked his lips and hesitated. He glanced quickly and nervously up and down the street. Unsurprisingly, no one paid them any mind. People were nattering on about the white smoke, with hands over their eyes, staring and pointing skyward, whispering gossip about the queen's shocking demise. The young man's hesitation and odd behavior just annoyed Niscene all the more.

"Have you a death wish?" she asked. The Sense took up a dark strain and Niscene reached out for it.

The question loosened the young man's lips. "Apologies, my lady," he said hastily. "Is your name not Niscene E'terrall?"

The Sense went wild and Niscene nearly choked on her tea. Who was this foolish young man? How did he know her name? No one in the capital knew her name. As it should be. No one ever would again. *The world will know not my face nor my name.* Niscene glanced at the cloud of smoke in the sky before responding. "Who are you?"

"He t-t-told me to t-talk only to Niscene E'terrall." The young man offered a weak smile then began backing away. "Said sh-she'd b-be here. B-b-but, if you're not her…"

"Wait," Niscene said, holding up her hand. The gesture froze the stammering fool in his place. "Who told you my name?"

The young man's face turned a ghostly white and he struggled in vain against his invisible bonds. "Please! I'm sorry! I didn't–"

The Sense hit a harsh note and Niscene's face darkened. Her annoyance building again, she forced the young man stock still. He yelped but she hushed him. Standing, she brought her face so close to his she could smell the fear on him. "Who told you about me?" she asked.

His pale eyes, pupils dilated in fear, flickered back and forth across the various clusters of people still pointing and whispering about the white smoke, as if trying to will someone to look in their direction to rescue him. His efforts proving unsuccessful, they fixed again on Niscene, who stared onyx-shaded daggers into him. The young man swallowed hard. "H-he gave me something f-for you." He swallowed again as sweat beaded down his forehead. "It's in m-m-my c-coat p-pocket."

Niscene arched an eyebrow, then her eyes focused on the young man's green coat. Without a second thought, she slipped a hand inside of it, searching for the pocket. She found it easily enough and extracted a scroll of parchment. It was the color of sandstone, with an inky black ribbon tied around it. A pulsating darkness issued from it.

Niscene's hands shook as she sat down again. Slowly, she set the parchment on the table in front of her, then stared, suddenly frightened, at the nervous young man.

"Who are you?" she demanded with false confidence.

"Open it," the young man said. All nervousness suddenly vanished from his demeanor. "He said you are to read it. You're to leave immediately."

Pressing her feet to the ground to steady herself, Niscene did her best to maintain her outward show of control. Inside, however, fear shook her. Carefully, she picked up the sandstone parchment and regarded it like an ancient artifact. Her eyes moved from it to the young man. She continued to stare at him, in a vain attempt to regain control of their exchange. She thought he might flinch, but he did not. His lips twitched upward into a knowing smile.

Averting her eyes, Niscene focused again on the parchment in her hands. Despite the fear that suddenly flooded into her, she felt a familiar presence invade her mind. Then, a summons – rather, a command. Even if she wanted to, she could not disobey. She fit a finger beneath the black ribbon. It fell to the ground as she slipped it off. When she unrolled the slip of parchment, Niscene's hands shook. Her face paled and her breath caught in her throat.

Written in a dark, twisted handwriting was a single name, much like one she had seen only once before. It felt almost a lifetime ago.

"Niscene E'terrall," said the familiar, fiery voice. Niscene's legs turned to jelly. Had she been standing, she would have fallen to the ground. *"You have done well."*

Slowly, Niscene lifted her eyes. The young man still sat in front of her, but his nervous mewling had completely evaporated. His soft blue eyes glowed a deep red and his lips twisted into a menacing smile. *"You are Morad'ash. Do what must be done."*

Though it came from the mouth of the light-haired young man, there was no mistaking that voice – or the command it gave. It was a voice she dared not disobey. A voice that burned in her skull and would do so forevermore. A voice that had brought down civilizations and changed the course of history for millennia. A voice of chaos and destruction. A voice that answered only to Death Herself.

The voice of Ash'an Rah.

EPILOGUE

AS WAS CUSTOMARY for queens, E'lisea was dressed in a marvelous, deep purple burial gown. Somehow it brought out the blue in her eyes. In this instance, however, her eyes were closed. The queen looked as though she had fallen asleep after a ball, too exhausted from a night of frivolity to undress. Despite his impeccable self-control, Dygon felt his lips curl into a smile. It had been known to happen on occasion.

Behind him, the steward felt the eyes of the assembled nobility, all who packed the rows of blue-toned pews for the queen's funeral. Paeter and the children already had paid their respects. Usually, Dygon was not one to draw attention to himself. Yet he lingered, taking his time for a moment with his sister.

Paeter misses you dearly. Or so it seemed. Dygon still could not discount the possibility that the king killed E'lisea. Though such a thought pained the steward, until he conclusively could prove the king did not commit the act, Dygon remained suspicious.

With a sigh, Dygon placed his hands on the edge of the casket; the gold was surprisingly cool despite the warmth of the violet incense the Philosophers had burned as part of the funeral ceremony. *The children miss you, as well, of course.* He blinked several times, attempting to clear away some of the ash that somehow had made it into his eyes. *As do I.*

Dygon stared at E'lisea's pale, cold face; not as fierce and defiant as when he saw her last. When he learned her secret. When she revealed she heard the Sense. E'lisea lay silent in the purple-lined casket, sleeping her eternal sleep. Usually a master of his emotions, Dygon clenched his jaw as a wave of agony and sadness washed over him, nearly cracking his carefully constructed mask.

Gripping tight the casket edge, Dygon closed his eyes and took a deep breath through his nostrils to compose himself. He knew what next he wished to say; it had occupied much of his time of late, had become an obsession, of sorts, and likely would continue to grow. But it would likely be a burden he would bear alone. For no one else would dare believe him; not without proof or evidence. And none was to be found, other than who lay before him.

Dygon then noticed a stray strand of E'lisea's strawberry blonde hair had managed to fall across her face. Absently, he moved to brush it aside. His fingers inadvertently touched the queen's cheek. So very cold. "What I wouldn't give to have one more moment with you, sweet sister," he whispered through unmoving lips.

"Words have power," Dygon recalled an old friend's warning. *"Use them wisely."*

Taking one last deep breath, Dygon opened his mouth and spoke, but only for his sister's ears, if by chance she still listened. "By the Maker above and all the gods of this world, I swear to you, my sweet sister: I will find the one who killed you."

ACKNOWLEDGMENTS

THIS LITTLE NOVELLA has been a long time coming, and not simply from my brain to my fingertips and to the screen. I've heard that a novel isn't written in a vacuum. Well, neither are novellas. Particularly this one.

To my early beta readers — Christine Niles, Chad Jones, Rena Burgess — my profuse and humble thanks. Your early input and insight into that initial draft helped me expand and flesh out the rest of what makes up Niscene and E'lisea's deliciously naughty tale.

To Chris Morris: Without your unceasing encouragement and year-long role as sounding board for new developments and scenes and ideas as I fleshed out – and fretted about – the story, I would not have published the damned thing at all. Your enthusiasm for this fantasy world I'm still discovering and uncovering gives me hope that, hey, maybe there are actual people out there interested in my stories. Thank you for your writing encouragement, but, most of all, thank you for your friendship. Though we've only known each other a few years, our friendship feels like one that has the depth of decades.

A huge shout-out of appreciation and gratitude to Cassandra Nicholson and Sonia Charry, whose encouraging feedback during our Phoenix Writers Group sessions always makes me feel better about my words.

To those secondary and tertiary characters and players (also known as friends and family) who support me in their own ways: Thank you.

I honestly have no idea where any of the story came from; but I'm glad to have written it. It may not be perfect (nothing ever is) but it's out in the world and nobody can take that from me. To the Creative Spirit, or the Muse, or Jesus in a piece of toast, or whoever buried the damn thing inside of me to begin with: Thank you. It's time to get cracking on the next one, so some inspiration would be most welcome.

Lastly but far from leastly: to my beloved wife and partner in crime and life, Nicole, to whom this novella is dedicated. You amaze me with your never-ending love for and support of and belief in me and my dream of hawking my fiction for a livin'. You help me discover a truer part of myself than I ever could alone. Only three words suffice and I'll repeat them over and over even long after I breathe my final breath: I love you.

About The Author

Tim Gallen lives and works in Phoenix, where he has no tan to speak of. He wrote and self-published an incredibly sappy and horrible novel over a decade ago while still in high school. He promises *Niscene's Creed* is a far better read. Feel free to stalk him on the Internet:

Twitter: @tim_gallen
Facebook: Tim Gallen Writes
Website: TimGallen.com